Title Withdrawn

OCT ' ' 2018   ED

"I NEED *ALL* OF YOU TO GO," MISS Z TOLD THEM, "and I need you to work as a team. The Civil War was still going on in 1863, remember. This could be dangerous. You may encounter trouble along the way. You'll need to work together and watch each other's backs. I know the four of you can. That's why I chose you. You're the Flashback Four."

David, Luke, Julia, and Isabel nodded. In the last hour they had gone from being four disinterested seventh graders to being a team with a mission to accomplish.

"We'll be witnessing history," Isabel said quietly. "And making it, too."

ALSO BY DAN GUTMAN

**And don't miss any of the books in the
My Weird School, My Weird School Daze,
My Weirder School, and My Weirdest School series!**

DAN GUTMAN

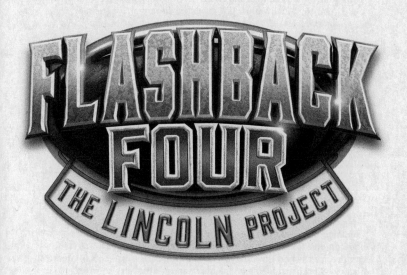

FLASHBACK FOUR

FOUR

THE LINCOLN PROJECT

HARPER

An Imprint of HarperCollinsPublishers

The author would like to acknowledge the following for use of photographs:
NASA, 16; © Paul Vathis/AP/Corbis, 49; Library of Congress, 67, 68;
Nina Wallace, 92; the Abraham Lincoln Presidential Library, 180.

Library of Congress Cataloging-in-Publication Data
Gutman, Dan.
 The Lincoln project / Dan Gutman. — First edition.
  pages cm. — (Flashback Four ; #1)
 Summary: "Miss Z, a mysterious billionaire and a collector of rare
photographs, is sending her four recruits back in time on a mission to
capture, for the first time, one of the most important moments in American
history—Abraham Lincoln giving his famous Gettysburg address"
—Provided by publisher.
 ISBN 978-0-06-237442-4
 [1. Time travel—Fiction. 2. Lincoln, Abraham, 1809–1865 Gettysburg
address—Fiction. 3. Photography—Fiction. 4. Adventure and
adventurers—Fiction.] I. Title.
PZ7.G9846Gj 2016   2015015557
[Fic]—dc23   CIP
                                                                             AC

Typography by Carla Weise
17 18 19 20 21   BVG   10 9 8 7 6 5 4 3 2
❖
First paperback edition, 2017

TO LIZA, ANDREW, AND ROSEMARY

THANKS TO:

Nina Wallace, David Lubar, Alan Kors,
Ray Dimetrosky, Craig Provorny, Howard Wolf,
Patty Mahoney Kropp, Zachary Lang,
Jennifer Mills-Knutsen, and Maura Jane Farrelly.

INTRODUCTION

"Four score and seven years ago . . ."

It is Thursday, November 19, 1863. Two o'clock in the afternoon. It's a warm day for autumn. President Abraham Lincoln stands tall over the speaker's platform. A huge crowd is spread out on the grassy hillside before him, watching him deliver perhaps the most memorable speech in American history. He speaks slowly and clearly.

". . . our fathers brought forth on this continent a new nation, conceived in liberty, and dedicated to

the proposition that all men are created equal. . . ."

Cheers and applause wash over the audience. Lincoln has to stop to wait until the noise dies down before he can continue. He wants the people to hear every word he has to say.

While the president speaks, four shadowy figures, who just arrived in Gettysburg the night before and are unknown to everyone in the crowd, push and elbow their way past onlookers.

"Now we are engaged in a great civil war, testing whether that nation, or any nation so conceived and so dedicated, can long endure. . . ."

It will be fifteen months until the war is over. Fifteen months until Americans will finally lay down their guns and stop killing one another. And fifteen months until one of them will pick up a gun and assassinate the president himself. Lincoln glances up briefly to scan the crowd before him, but doesn't notice anything unusual.

"We are met on a great battlefield of that war. We have come to dedicate a portion of that field, as

a final resting place for those who here gave their lives that that nation might live. It is altogether fitting and proper that we should do this. . . ."

The four figures strain to hear the president's words. They feel a sense of urgency as they try to get close enough to the stage. They won't have a lot of time to complete their mission. They, and they alone, know that the president's speech will be very short. Two hundred seventy words, give or take a few. In two short minutes, it will all be over. They have to act fast.

"But, in a larger sense, we can not dedicate—we can not consecrate—we can not hallow—this ground. The brave men, living and dead, who struggled here, have consecrated it, far above our poor power to add or detract. . . ."

One of the conspirators, a boy, holds a small device in his hand. It's a strange-looking thing, or at least it's strange-looking to the people who might have noticed it that day. Silvery and metallic, it's small enough to fit in one hand, but powerful enough to change every history book ever written.

"The world will little note, nor long remember what we say here, but it can never forget what they did here. . . ."

The young man fiddles with the device in his hand. Something seems to be wrong. It's not working. He stops moving forward. Time is running out. Droplets of sweat slide down his forehead. His hands have become slippery.

"It is for us the living, rather, to be dedicated here to the unfinished work which they who fought here have thus far so nobly advanced. . . ."

The young man gnashes his teeth. *What's the problem?* he asks himself. He has to solve it. And fast. After all the preparation they have been through, it can't end now. If he fails in this mission, all will have been for nothing.

"It is rather for us to be here dedicated to the great task remaining before us—that from these honored dead we take increased devotion to that cause for which they gave the last full measure of devotion . . ."

There are only a few seconds left. The young man's companions surround him, imploring him to figure out what's wrong with the device. He fiddles some more with the buttons, trying anything to make it work.

"that we here highly resolve that these dead shall not have died in vain—that this nation, under God, shall have a new birth of freedom . . ."

Finally, for reasons unexplained, the device turns on. It seems to be working to the young man's satisfaction. He holds it up in the air over his head. He points it in the direction of the president.

"and that government of the people, by the people, for the people, shall not perish from the . . ."

As Abraham Lincoln speaks the final word of the Gettysburg Address, the boy pushes the button.

THE YELLOW ENVELOPES

EVERY STORY SHOULD START AT THE BEGINNING, of course. As the old song goes, it's *a very good place to start*.

This particular story begins in Boston, Massachusetts, and it takes place, oddly enough, in the present day. Or it *starts* in the present day, anyway. My apologies for not providing you with the exact year, but by the time you read this book, that year will very possibly have come and gone. Suffice to say, our story begins *now*. Let's call it four o'clock in the afternoon, shortly after school has let out for the day.

There are four main characters you'll need to keep

track of as you read this story, but it shouldn't be that difficult. Two girls, two boys. They're all native Bostonians of approximately the same age—twelve years old.

Julia comes from an affluent family and attends the expensive, private, all-girls Winsor School, a short walk from Fenway Park.

Luke has more humble roots and lives in the Dorchester section of town. His parents are both long-time members of the Boston Police Department.

David—tall, thin, and athletic—is a good student but is more interested in cracking jokes than books.

Isabel is quite bookish, serious, and eager to succeed.

David, Isabel, Julia, and Luke have never met before this day, but circumstances beyond their control will bring them together, as you're about to see.

David Williams was shooting hoops with some friends at Medal of Honor Park near East First Street. He came out to the park most days after school looking for a game. Usually, he found one with teenagers a few years older. On this particular day, he had just poured in a jump shot from the top of the key when everybody decided to take a water break. As David toweled off his face, a middle-aged man in a suit and tie leaned over the bench where David was sitting.

"Excuse me," the man said. "Is your name David Williams?"

"Yeah, so what?"

David turned around and eyed the well-dressed man suspiciously. Was he a cop? A crazy person? Maybe he was a college recruiter. They scout kids really young these days.

The man handed David a yellow envelope, then turned on his heel and left without saying another word.

At almost the same time, Isabel Alvarez was doing her homework at a corner desk on the third floor of the Boston Public Library on Boylston Street. She usually came to this spot because it was quiet and she wouldn't be bothered by her family, or by giggly classmates who would rather socialize and gossip than get their schoolwork done. Isabel worked hard at her studies, having come to accept the conventional wisdom that hard work leads to a high grade point average, which leads to a smart mind, which leads to a good college, which leads to a high-paying job, which leads to a successful life.

She was deeply immersed in solving an algebraic equation with one variable when a man in a suit and tie tapped her on the shoulder, startling her.

"Excuse me," the man whispered. "Is your name Isabel Alvarez?"

"Yes. Is something wrong?"

The man didn't reply. He simply reached into his jacket pocket, pulled out a yellow envelope, handed it to her, and left.

Minutes later, Luke Borowicz was banging away on an old Ms. Pac-Man machine at the little grocery store on Washington Street around the corner from his house. Luke was a stocky boy with floppy brown hair, and he was wearing his favorite Red Sox T-shirt. He came to this store a lot, and seven of the top ten scores on the machine were immortalized with his initials. The game relaxed him. Even though he had been diagnosed with mild ADD several years earlier, Luke found that he could focus his attention like a laser when it came to things that interested him, like old arcade games.

Luke had just broken through the 300,000-point

mark when he noticed the reflection of a man in a suit and tie on the screen.

"Excuse me," the man said. "Is your name Luke Borowicz?"

"Uh-huh," Luke said, without turning around. "What can I do for you?"

The man put a yellow envelope on the console and silently walked away.

Several minutes later, Julia Brennan was at the Urban Outfitters store in nearby Harvard Square with two girlfriends. She had a dance coming up in a few weeks, and she'd already tried on five dresses. Her father had given her a hundred dollars to spend, even though he saw no reason why Julia couldn't wear one of the dresses she already had in her closet. He also saw no reason why a girl of Julia's age should be going to dances in the first place. He lamented over how fast his kids were growing up. Before she'd left the house that morning, Julia had rolled her eyes and told him, "You wouldn't understand."

Now, as she came out of the fitting room, a man in a suit and tie approached her.

"Excuse me," the man said. "Is your name Julia Brennan?"

"Who wants to know?" she replied, instinctively taking a step back and glancing left and right for exits.

"If your name is Julia Brennan, this is for you," the man said, holding out a yellow envelope.

Julia took it. The man nodded, turned, and walked away without saying another word.

All four of the kids had received their envelope within five minutes. Each of them tore it open and read the sheet of paper tucked inside. . . .

CONGRATULATIONS!

You are invited to participate in a very special, once-in-a-lifetime experience. Please join me at 4:30 p.m. today. No RSVP necessary. We will hold your place for thirty minutes only. Address: John Hancock Tower, 200 Clarendon Street, Boston. Twenty-third floor. Pasture Company. Please do not share this invitation or discuss it with anyone.

That's all it said. There was no phone number to call. No email address. No closing, and no signature. There was no indication of what one might encounter if one followed the instructions and went to the address. It could be a party, a concert, or some sort of a sporting event, maybe. Most likely, they all figured, it was a scam.

Most people would throw an invitation like that away. But each envelope did include one small entice- ment to increase the chance that it would get noticed. Paper-clipped to each invitation were four crisp five- dollar bills.

David read his invitation a second time. He held the bills up to the sun and determined that they were legit. Then he took out his cell phone to check the time. It was already four minutes after four o'clock. There was just enough time to get to the John Han- cock Tower.

David stuffed the bills in his pocket, said good-bye to his friends at the basketball court, and hopped on his bike. It was a quick ride to the Hancock Tower.

Why would somebody give me twenty bucks for doing nothing? he wondered as he pedaled down Har- rison Avenue. *There's gotta be a catch.*

When David got to the Hancock, a sixty-story sky- scraper, he locked his bike to a street sign and walked over to the front door.

Isabel was already inside the Hancock, waiting in the lobby. She liked to arrive at places early so she could decompress and get her bearings before any social event. It helped calm her down. Also, she felt that being early for an appointment was the right thing to do. People who show up late for things are inconsiderate, she believed.

Moments later, Julia and Luke came from opposite directions, nearly bumping into each other as they passed through the big revolving door.

All four of them—David, Luke, Julia, and Isabel—surrounded by a group of well-dressed twenty-somethings, squeezed into an elevator and rode it up to the twenty-third floor. When the doors opened, they were the only ones who got out.

Luke looked around the hallway suspiciously. Only once in his life had he been inside a fancy office building like this. The sign on the wall behind the front desk read PASTURE COMPANY.

Julia looked around. There was no clue as to what kind of a company this was, or why she had been summoned to this particular spot at this time.

When the glass door to the waiting area buzzed open, all four of them approached the front desk. A nameplate read MRS. ELLA VADER. The receptionist looked up from her computer and smiled.

"Ah, you made it! Splendid!" Mrs. Vader said. "We've been waiting for you."

PICTURES ON A WALL

YOU'RE PROBABLY WONDERING WHY THESE FOUR kids were summoned to this office in the Hancock Tower. Patience, reader.

David, Julia, Isabel, and Luke cast sidelong glances at one another, each wondering if the rest of them already knew one another.

"Is this gonna take long?" David asked the receptionist.

"I'd say an hour or so should do it," replied Mrs. Vader. "If you would all take a seat, we'll get started shortly."

While the others sat down, Luke paced around

the waiting room. He didn't like sitting. It made him nervous.

None of the kids had spoken a word to the other three yet. Awkward silence hung in the air. Julia sighed, pulled out her cell phone, and began texting her friends. David picked up a copy of *Sports Illustrated* from the coffee table in front of him and leafed mindlessly through the pages. Isabel looked around anxiously.

The wall of the waiting room was filled with dozens of eight-by-ten photos, framed and lined up perfectly. Luke went over to take a closer look.

Each photo depicted a dramatic moment in history. Astronaut Buzz Aldrin standing on the moon. The mushroom cloud from the first atomic test blowing up over the New Mexico desert. Ecstatic young Germans tearing down the Berlin Wall. The *Hindenburg* erupting into flames over Lakehurst, New Jersey.

A few of the events depicted in the photos were familiar to Luke. Most of them had taken place long before he was born and didn't mean much to him.

"Follow me, please," Mrs. Vader said to the group.

She ushered them into a large office, invited them to sit down again, and left. There were more photos on the walls here. American soldiers rushing the beaches of Normandy on D-Day. A lone protestor holding up a long line of tanks at Tiananmen Square in China. Lots of famous faces—Franklin Delano Roosevelt, John F. Kennedy, Jackie Robinson, James Dean, Marilyn Monroe.

In the middle of the wall was one empty rectangle where a photo had either fallen off or been removed, been stolen, or perhaps borrowed temporarily. A visitor's eye was drawn not so much to the famous photos on the wall, but to the one spot that didn't have one.

On the other side of the room was a large white-board, like one of those smartboards you've seen in your school. It was connected to a laptop computer on a cart, and also to a projector that hung down from the ceiling. The board itself was on wheels, so it could be moved around.

In the center of the room was a huge desk, carved

from dark, heavy wood. There were only a few papers and knickknacks on it. It was almost *too* neat. This was the desk of a man who didn't have enough to do. There was no chair behind the desk, which was odd. But none of the kids noticed that.

They couldn't *help* but notice the prism-shaped nameplate at the edge of the desk. It had an unusual name on it—CHRIS ZANDERGOTH.

After a few minutes of looking around awkwardly, it became impossible for the four of them to avoid eye contact with one another. David was the first to break the silence.

"Anybody know why we're here?" he asked.

"Nope," Luke replied.

"I got this invitation," Isabel volunteered, taking it out of her pocket.

"Me too," said Julia.

"It's like a golden ticket," David said. "I feel like Willy Wonka's gonna come walking in here and take us to his chocolate factory."

At that moment, the door opened and a woman in a wheelchair rolled into the room.

"Welcome!" she said cheerfully. "I'm Chris, and I'm so glad you were able to join me this afternoon."

Although we've come a long way in the last fifty

years, here in the twenty-first century, most of us still assume that any rich, powerful person is a man. But Chris Zandergoth, the CEO of Pasture Company, was a woman.

CHAPTER 3

ONE MOMENT IN TIME

CHRIS ZANDERGOTH WAS FORTYISH, WITH A round face and dark eyes. She was dressed in a conservative business suit. She appeared to be a tall woman, although it was hard to tell because she was sitting in a wheelchair.

"You must be David," she said, locking eyes and putting out her hand. "And I guess you're Isabel."

After shaking hands with all four of the children, she wheeled herself around to the other side of the desk.

"I know Zandergoth is a mouthful," she said. "My friends call me Miss Z, and I hope you will, too. Have you heard of me? Do you know my name?"

"No," murmured the group.

"Good," Miss Z said. "I'd hate to be a celebrity. Can you imagine enjoying a meal at your favorite restaurant, and having to stop every five minutes to autograph some scrap of paper? I wouldn't enjoy that one bit."

"Your photos are cool," said Julia. "Did you take them yourself?"

David rolled his eyes. *Is this girl some kind of a dope?* he thought. *Does she really think this Zandergoth lady took the picture of that astronaut on the moon?*

"No," Miss Z said, smiling. "Photography is a hobby, a *passion*, of mine. Well, *collecting* photos more than shooting them. I think it's human nature to collect things, don't you? We seem to have this curious desire to hang on to material objects. We must derive some degree of pleasure from accumulating stuff. You all probably collect something, am I right?"

"I collect glass horses," said Isabel.

"I collect Pez dispensers," said David.

"I don't collect anything," said Luke.

"I like to collect money," said Julia, provoking some good-natured chuckling.

"Don't we all?" Miss Z said. She turned her chair around and rolled closer to the wall of photos, pointing up at one of them.

"I'm a history buff myself," Miss Z said. "See this photo? Do you have any idea why it's significant? It doesn't look very historical. Why would I have it up on my wall?"

David, Julia, Luke, and Isabel studied the photo. There was nothing special about it. Just an old-time street scene.

"Give up?" Miss Z asked. "This was the first photo

ever taken that had a person in it. See those men in the lower left corner? One appears to be shining the shoes of the other one. This picture was taken in Paris during the spring of 1838. Before that instant in time, no human being had ever been photographed."

Miss Z gazed at the photo, letting her words sink in. She was fascinated by the idea that none of the millions of people who had lived before that moment had ever been preserved in a photographic image.

"Very interesting," Isabel said, and she wasn't just saying that to butter up a grown-up. She had always been interested in history, and social studies was her favorite subject.

"Yeah, but why are we here?" David asked, glancing at the clock on the wall. "I have practice tonight."

"Is this a job interview or something?" asked Julia.

"Or is this some kind of a scam?" asked Luke, who was never one to mince words.

Luke didn't trust Chris Zandergoth, no matter how fancy her office was. In Luke's short lifetime, he had already figured out that almost every grown-up he'd met was running some kind of a game.

"Oh, it's no scam," Miss Z replied. "Let me ask you a question. Do you kids like adventure?"

"Depends on the adventure," replied Luke.

"Good answer!" said Miss Z. "Well, I hope you *do* like adventure, because that's the reason why I asked you to come here today. I'd like to send you on the adventure of a lifetime."

I CHOSE YOU
VERY CAREFULLY

"WILL YOU EXCUSE ME FOR A MOMENT?" MISS Zandergoth asked the kids. "I need to go to the little girls' room."

David shot a glance at the others. *Little girls' room?* Who says *that*?

As soon as Miss Z wheeled herself out of the room and closed the bathroom door behind her, all four kids whipped out their cell phones and Googled "Chris Zandergoth."

"Got 'er," Luke whispered. "She's thirty-nine. The picture on Wikipedia looks just like her."

"Born in Palo Alto, California," said Isabel.

"It says here that she's a *billionaire*," said Julia, impressed. Anybody who had a lot of money was impressive to Julia.

"Check it out!" exclaimed David. "She's the one who started Findamate.com, that online dating service."

In a matter of seconds, they had gathered enough information about Chris Zandergoth to write a term paper.

Miss Zandergoth, they discovered, was a computer prodigy who'd dropped out of Stanford University after two years to start Findamate. The site took off, and by the time she was twenty, she was a millionaire several times over. By the time she was thirty, she was one of the richest women in America.

What the kids did *not* discover online was exactly how Findamate had become so successful. Instead of relying on the typical questionnaires to help people find their "love match," Zandergoth had figured out how to hack into the computers of the National Security Agency.

As you may or may not know, reader, the NSA was founded to fight terrorism by monitoring information. After 9/11 the NSA began a secret mass surveillance program in which they scooped up data from cell phones, emails, and text messages sent by ordinary Americans.

While the NSA was spying on every man, woman, and child in America, the agency never suspected that Chris Zandergoth was spying on *them*. By tapping into the NSA database, she was able to match up like-minded people much better than PerfectDate, LoveBug, or any other online dating service. Best of all, she was able to get away with it, because the NSA was too embarrassed to admit their own computers had been hacked. To this day, the American public has no knowledge of this secret. You're reading it here for the first time.

But as far as David, Julia, Isabel, and Luke were concerned, Chris Zandergoth simply started a hugely successful online dating service.

"Online dating is creepy," said Isabel.

"Maybe we should get out of here," said Julia.

The two girls were about to head for the door when they heard the toilet flush.

"What's she gonna do?" David asked. "There are four of us and one of her."

"I don't feel good about this," Isabel whispered, getting back in her seat.

The bathroom door opened and Miss Zandergoth rolled out into the office.

"So," she said cheerfully, "have you finished Googling me?"

The kids laughed, trying to put their phones away without being too obvious about it.

"I figured that letting you kids do a little research would be a lot easier than telling you my own boring life story," Miss Z continued. "By now you know how I started Findamate. The *Huffington Post* said I've been responsible for more marriages than anyone in the world. That should be in the *Guinness Book of World Records*, don't you think?"

Luke looked at Miss Zandergoth's desk again. He noticed that there were no framed photos of her family. For a woman who had helped so many people find love, it looked like she had never found the perfect match for herself.

"What does any of this have to do with *us*?" asked Isabel.

"Yeah, did you bring us here to fix us up with each other?" asked David.

Julia glanced at the boys and giggled nervously.

"No, not at all," Miss Z said, leaning her head back

to laugh. "But I do know for a fact that the four of you will work well together. You would be amazed at how powerful my software algorithms are. I chose you *very* carefully."

"Oh, I can see that," David said. "Two boys. Two girls. I guess you picked me because you needed a black kid."

"I suppose I'm the token Hispanic," said Isabel.

"What, no Asian?" asked Luke. "How do you expect to win Multicultural Humanitarian of the Year?"

"Very funny," said Miss Z. "I matched up your personalities, your likes, your dislikes, your strengths, and your weaknesses. I chose you for your compatibility, not your ethnicity."

"How do you know so much about us?" asked Julia.

"Oh, nothing is private anymore, my dear," Miss Z replied. "You should know that. Americans gave up their privacy the day we accepted cell phones."

Julia thought of all the information stored on the phone in her handbag—all the photos, texts, and private messages she shared with her friends. Maybe this lady had seen them all.

"Oh, don't worry," Miss Z continued, "I assure you that your crushes and selfies are of no interest to me. I have far more important concerns. But I promised you an adventure, and that's what I hope to deliver."

"So what's the adventure?" Luke asked.

"Well, let me ask you this, Luke. Do you like history, or as I guess you call it, social studies?"

"It's okay," Luke replied. The others mumbled similar noncommittal responses, not wanting to go out on a limb until they'd heard more.

"Then tell me, what's the most significant thing that ever happened in *your* history?" Miss Z asked.

The four of them thought about it.

"I went to Disney World for my tenth birthday," Isabel said.

"I broke both of my arms in second grade when I fell off the monkey bars," said David.

"I scored a million points at Centipede once," said Luke.

"Some guy once gave me an envelope with twenty bucks in it," said Julia, provoking a laugh.

"That's it, huh? Don't you find that sad?" asked Miss Z. She waved her arm toward the photos all over the walls. "Look around you. Don't our lives seem trivial and dull compared with all these amazing moments? We only get to hang around this silly planet for about eighty short years. Shouldn't we be allowed to have at least *one* truly memorable moment in that time?"

"Yeah, I suppose," Luke said.

"Well, most people can only dream about what I'm going to offer you. This will dwarf anything you will ever do for the rest of your lives."

CHAPTER 5

THE SMARTEST SMARTBOARD

THE RECEPTIONIST, MRS. VADER, KNOCKED ON the door and brought in a platter full of cookies, little cakes, and other treats. She poured a cup of tea for Miss Z and set the platter down on her desk. Then she left the room.

"We don't know you," David said, eyeing the platter suspiciously. "Why should we trust you? Because you gave us twenty bucks and some sweets?"

"You *shouldn't* trust me," Miss Z admitted, taking a cookie. "It's *good* that you don't trust me. That shows that you're smart. I could be anybody. But I'm *not* anybody."

"Yeah, you're a super-rich lady," said Julia, picking up a brownie and taking a bite. "That doesn't mean we should trust you more than any stranger we met on the street."

When Julia didn't topple over dead, the others took treats off the platter.

"So what's the big adventure?" Isabel asked, nibbling a pastry.

"Is it dangerous?" asked Julia.

"It could be," Miss Z replied. "I won't lie to you."

"Will we have to do anything illegal?" David asked.

"Definitely not," Miss Z replied. "I would never ask you to break a law."

"I need some more details before I commit to anything," said Luke.

"Smart boy," said Miss Z. "I'm glad I chose you four."

"Here's what I want to know," David asked. "What's in it for us? Do we get paid?"

"Paid?" Miss Z looked hurt. "For the adventure of a lifetime? You should pay *me*!"

"Well, what's in it for *you*?" David asked. "Money, right?"

"Young man, money is the least of my concerns," Miss Z said, looking David in the eye. "Believe me, I have achieved my financial goals *many* times over."

"Look, I'm not in the mood for guessing games," Luke said, getting to his feet. "What's the big adventure? Tell me right now, or I walk."

"Okay, okay," Miss Z said as she put down her teacup and pulled her wheelchair back from the desk.

She rolled over to the smartboard on the other side of the room, admiring it for a moment. David, Isabel, Julia, and Luke turned to face her. They had been wondering why a wealthy businesswoman would have a smartboard in her office.

"When I was a kid, we had plain old blackboards in school," Miss Z said. "The teacher would write on the board with chalk. Do you even know what chalk *is*?"

"Yeah," Julia replied. "When I was little, I would draw pictures with it on the sidewalk."

"At some point," continued Miss Z, "they got rid of those old blackboards and replaced them with *white*boards. You'd write on them with erasable markers. No chalk dust! No mess. And now, of course, a lot of schools have replaced their whiteboards with smartboards, which interface with a computer and a projector. You can type on the computer, draw pictures, go online, and interact with the board like a computer screen."

"Yeah, yeah, we know all that," Luke said. "So?"

"Well," said Miss Z, "now we have *this*."

She gazed at the board again, almost lovingly.

"It looks like *any* smartboard," said David.

"But it's *not* like any smartboard," said Miss Z. "It's a *smarter* board. I call it simply the Board. It makes a regular smartboard look like a *dumbboard*. In fact, I'd go so far as to say this is the smartest smartboard in the *world*. I've spent the last ten years of my life perfecting this technology, and I spent hundreds of millions of dollars on it. If it were to fall into the wrong hands, it could be used for any number of nefarious purposes."

Isabel looked up the word *nefarious* on her smart-phone.

"What does it do?" David asked.

"I'm sure you kids understand that we're sur-rounded by invisible fields of force at all times. Like TV and radio signals. They move through the air in waves."

"Microwaves, too," added Luke.

"Right," said Miss Z, "and I'm sure you also real-ize that as the earth turns around, we're constantly in motion. Even though it seems like we're in one place, we're all moving faster than a jet plane right now. What you may *not* know is that light travels at a constant speed of 186,000 miles per second," Miss Z explained. "It's sort of like a cosmic speed limit, which we call the speed of light. It works out to about 671 million miles per hour."

"Your point?" asked Luke.

"Think about it," said Miss Z. "The moon is about 240,000 miles away from the earth. So when you look out the window and see the moon, you're not seeing the moon as it is *now*. You're seeing the moon as it was a little over a second ago. In a way, you've traveled through time."

"Slow down," David said. "Are you telling us you've built yourself a time machine?"

"You might say that, yes," replied Miss Z. "I'm not very good at explaining this stuff in simple terms."

I know what you're thinking, reader. Either Miss Z is some kind of a genius, or this is some kind of a prank. Well, I won't keep you in suspense. She's a genius.

"You turned a smartboard into a machine that can send people through time?" asked Isabel, incredulous.

"That sums it up nicely, yes."

"Oh, come on!" Luke said. "That's bull! That's science fiction stuff."

"I can understand why you would say that, Luke," Miss Z said. "It seems too fantastic to be true. But remember, robots were the stuff of science fiction before we figured out how to build them. Space travel was science fiction before we figured out how to do it. Just about any advanced technology was science fiction before it became reality."

"And you figured out how to do this?" asked Luke.

"Look," replied Miss Z, "if a human being could move at the speed of light, any number of paradoxes would become possible. Space time is warped by the gravity of a black hole, for instance. If you fell into a black hole, you would appear at another place and time in the universe. Einstein said nobody can travel faster than the speed of light. But space can stretch, shrink, or be deformed. And when that happens, time is deformed, too. Space and time are two aspects of the same thing—space-time. It can deform enough to carry you anywhere at any speed. Black holes are tunnels through the universe. Am I making any sense at all?"

"So you can send somebody into a black hole?" asked Isabel.

"I don't buy it," David said, shaking his head. "That's crazy."

"Still sounds like a lot of mumbo jumbo to me," said Luke.

"Look, I could spend the next hour explaining the nuts and bolts of this technology," Miss Z told the group. "But I have a better idea. David, let's assume for a moment that I *have* created a time machine, and you could use it to travel back to any date and place in history. Where would you go?"

David thought it over for a minute.

"Any time in history?" he finally said. "I'd go back to the day Wilt Chamberlain scored a hundred points in a single NBA game. It would be cool to see that."

"A hundred points in one game?" asked Luke. "Now *that's* crazy. I know that Michael Jordan's high game was sixty-nine points, and that was only because the game went into overtime."

"It *happened*," David insisted. "My dad told me about it. He doesn't lie. Wilt Chamberlain scored a hundred points. And it wasn't in overtime."

"Of all the things in history to witness, *that's* what you choose?" asked Julia. "Who cares about some silly basketball game?"

"I care," David said. "What would *you* do, travel back in time to witness the opening of the first Abercrombie & Fitch store?"

Julia looked hurt.

"Please don't argue, children," said Miss Z as she rolled over to her computer. "I specifically matched you four up because I thought you would get along. David, when was that basketball game, exactly?"

"I don't know," David replied. "Before I was born. Nineteen sixties, I think."

Isabel looked it up on her smartphone. It only took a few seconds to get the answer.

"It was March 2, 1962," she said. "The game took place at the Hershey Sports Arena in Hershey, Pennsylvania."

"Thank you, Isabel," said Miss Z. "David, would you mind going over there and standing in front of the Board, please?"

"What are you gonna do to me?" he asked nervously. "Zap me with laser beams?"

"No. I'm going to send you to the Hershey Sports Arena on March 2, 1962."

"That's nuts," David insisted, still sitting in his chair.

"Well, if it's nuts, then it won't work, right?" asked Miss Z. "Nothing will happen. I'll look like a fool. So you have nothing to lose. Would you just go stand over there in front of the Board for a moment?"

"Go ahead," Luke said. "Do it, dude. It'll be funny."

David got up reluctantly and stood in front of the Board.

"Closer, please," said Miss Z. "Your body must be within two feet of the surface."

"This is wack," David said as he moved closer to the Board.

"Have fun, David!" said Isabel.

"Yeah, nice knowin' you," said Julia.

"Okay," said Miss Z as she typed something on her computer. "Are you ready, David?"

"Yeah, ready for *nothing*," he replied.

Miss Z typed a few more commands and hit the Enter key. There was a brief buzzing sound, and then the screen on the Board lit up. Five bands of color appeared, and after a few seconds they merged together to form one band of intense white light. It appeared to stretch out and away from the surface of the Board until it reached David. He put up one hand to shield his eyes.

"What's going on?" he asked. "It's so bright!"

"You'll see in a moment," said Miss Z. "Better close your eyes."

"Is he okay?" asked Julia, frightened.

"We are circumventing the first commandment of relativity!" shouted an excited Miss Z. "The laws of physics now make it possible to warp the matter and energy of the observable universe! Light, time, and space are combined in a whirling magnetic field!"

There was an intense humming sound, a low frequency rumbling like a diesel engine idling.

David appeared to be flickering, like the image on a television screen just before a power outage. He was clicking on and off.

"What's happening to him?" asked Isabel, alarmed.

"Stop it!" shouted Julia. "Turn it off!"

"What the—"

And with that, David was gone.

CHAPTER 6

IT WORKS!

FOR A FEW SECONDS, LUKE, ISABEL, AND JULIA just sat there with startled looks on their faces.

"Where *is* he?" Isabel asked. "What happened to him?"

"I told you what happened to him," said Miss Z. "He's gone."

"This isn't funny," said Julia.

"It's a trick," said Luke, getting up to investigate. "He's hiding behind the Board."

Luke looked behind the Board, then got down on his knees to check under the furniture. But David was nowhere to be seen.

"The trick was to warp space-time!" Miss Z said triumphantly. "David is exactly where he wanted to be."

Miss Z was absolutely right. On March 2 in 1962, David opened his eyes and found himself standing on the steps outside the Hershey Sports Arena in Hershey, Pennsylvania.

TONIGHT, the sign read, NEW YORK KNICKS VS. PHILADELPHIA WARRIORS.

"Oh man!" David exclaimed. "You *gotta* be kidding me!"

It was dark outside the arena, and cold. A slight rain was falling. A roar could be heard inside, and David climbed the steps to follow the sound. There was a ticket booth, but nobody was in it. There was no need to sell tickets anymore. The game was almost over.

David pinched himself to make sure he was real. He walked around in a daze, almost bumping into a lone janitor sweeping the floor with a long broom.

"You okay, sonny?" the janitor asked.

"Yeah," David mumbled. "Hey, what year is it?"

"Nineteen sixty-two, of course," the man replied. "You *sure* you're okay? Need me to call a doctor?"

David waved him off and pulled open the door that led inside the arena. The roar grew tenfold. The crowd was on its feet, so he couldn't see what the people were so excited about. But he could make a pretty good guess.

"Wilt! Wilt! Wilt!" people were chanting.

The Hershey Arena was small. It still is. It holds about eight thousand fans, and it was half full on this night. There were plenty of empty seats. As David made his way down the steps toward the court, he wondered why two NBA teams would be playing in such a rinky-dink arena.

In fact, the league was only in its sixteenth season that year. Professional basketball was not a major sport at the time, and the NBA would play occasional games outside of big cities to attract new fans. There were no TV cameras around the court, no giant video screens overhead. The game wasn't televised.

David instantly noticed another big difference in the game—only a few of the players on the court were black. In 1962, there were only thirty-seven black players in the whole league.

"Give it to Wilt!" the crowd chanted. "Give it to Wilt!"

David spotted an open seat ten rows up from the court and slipped into that row, trying to be inconspicuous in case the security guards might be checking for tickets. Standing next to him was a boy, about ten years old, wearing a Philadelphia jacket. He was holding a program in one hand and a pencil in the other. The program had a photo of Wilt Chamberlain on the cover.

"How many points does Chamberlain have?" David asked.

"Ninety-one!" the boy shouted over the crowd noise. Then he showed David what he had written in his program. "Wilt had twenty-three points in the first quarter, forty-one at half time, and sixty-nine at the end of the third quarter. Did you ever see anything like this in your whole life?"

"Not me," David replied. "That's for sure."

Down on the court, Wilt Chamberlain was standing at the foul line. He was a huge man—seven feet one inch tall, weighing 280 pounds. And this was in an era when basketball players were smaller than they are today.

A little background, reader. Wilton Norman Chamberlain was called "Wilt the Stilt," or sometimes "The Big Dipper." He wore number thirteen. David knew that Wilt played for the Philadelphia Warriors before they moved to California. In 1963, the Philadelphia 76ers were born.

The referee flipped Wilt the ball. He was one of the few players who shot free throws underhand, and he was also notoriously *bad* at it, averaging about 50 percent over his career. But not on this night. When all was said and done, he would sink twenty-eight foul shots in thirty-two attempts.

Wilt took a deep breath and made the shot, bouncing it off the backboard and into the net.

"Ninety-two!" shouted the boy next to David, along with about a thousand other fans.

David watched, enthralled, as the Knicks dribbled the ball downcourt. He wasn't thinking about how he got there, or how he was going to get back home. All he was thinking about was that there were two minutes and twelve seconds left on the clock, and Wilt had eight more points to score. How was he going to pull *that* off?

"A hundred! A hundred!" the crowd began to chant, urging Wilt on.

"He's gonna do it," David said to the boy next to him. "It's a lock."

"No way!" the boy replied. "Eight points in two minutes? It's impossible."

"Wanna bet?" David asked holding out his hand. "If Wilt *doesn't* score a hundred, I'll give you ten bucks."

"And what if he *does* score a hundred?" the boy asked. "What do I have to give *you*?"

"How about you give me your program?" David said.

"You got a bet!" the boy replied, and they shook on it.

The Knicks were passing the ball back and forth as they moved slowly downcourt, trying to burn seconds off the clock. They knew what was going on. No team wants to be known for giving up a hundred points to one guy, so they were doing their best to stall for time.

Finally, one of the Warriors intentionally fouled the Knick with the ball. The guy made the shot, but the score didn't matter anymore. The Warriors were ahead by over twenty points. All that mattered was getting the ball back, and getting it to Wilt so he could put up another shot.

Wilt was double- and triple-teamed as the Warriors took possession, but nobody could stop him. Somehow, Wilt's teammates got the ball to him close to the basket. He dribbled twice, spun around with those big elbows pushing the Knicks out of his way, and launched a fadeaway that dropped gently into the net without touching the rim.

"Ninety-four!" four thousand people screamed.

There were less than two minutes left on the clock now. Wilt looked exhausted as he backpedaled down-court. The Knicks were trying to run out the clock again, but one of them got sloppy and a Warrior stole the ball from him. He could have taken an easy lay-up himself, but he didn't. He slowed things down, waiting for Wilt to get into position under the basket. Defend-ers were all over the big man, but he had a height advantage over them. The Warrior with the ball lofted up a lob pass. Wilt leaped to grab it, came down, and then jumped up again to jam the ball through the hoop.

"Ninety-six!" four thousand people screamed.

"It's a Dipper Dunk!" shouted the boy next to David as they both jumped up and down.

Wilt was also fouled on the play, so he got two free throws.

"Ninety-seven!" four thousand people screamed when he made the first one.

"Ninety-eight!" four thousand people screamed when he made the second one.

Now there was a minute left in the game. The clock seemed to be ticking down faster, and the fans started counting it down.

"Fifty-nine! Fifty-eight! Fifty-seven . . ."

Wilt needed just one more basket. The Knicks had the ball, but one of the Warriors committed a foul right away to get possession back.

After the missed foul shot, the Warriors brought the ball downcourt again.

"Forty-nine! Forty-eight! Forty-seven . . ."

Wilt set up in the post. Everybody knew what was going to happen next. The Warriors would try to get the ball to Wilt so he could take one last shot. There were Knicks all over him. They weren't guarding any of the other Warriors.

Miraculously, a bounce pass found its way into Wilt's hands. He didn't risk a dribble that might be stolen. He leaped up and shot.

Miss. The ball bounced hard off the rim. One of the Warriors got the rebound. The crowd was going crazy. The calmest person in the arena was David, because he was the only one who knew what was going to happen.

Wilt got the pass again and took another shot.

He missed *again*! Forty-four seconds left now.

Once again, the Warriors rebounded.

They passed it to Wilt a *third* time.

There were five Knicks sticking their hands in his face and trying to strip the ball from him.

Wilt muscled away from them, took one step, and jumped.

He shoots. He scores!

"A hundred!" four thousand people screamed.

For the first time in history—and the *only* time in history—a player had scored a hundred points in an NBA game. And it hadn't even gone into overtime.

The crowd, needless to say, went wild. People were throwing papers up in the air and storming the court. Grown-ups wanted to shake Wilt Chamberlain's hand. Kids wanted to clap him on the back, or simply touch him.

"I *told* you it was a lock," David said to the boy next to him.

"You were right," the boy replied, handing David his program. Giving it away didn't bother him very much. He had witnessed an historic moment that he would never forget, something he could tell his children and grandchildren about someday. David rolled up the program and stuck it in his back pocket.

There was just one problem. There were still twenty seconds left on the clock. Unless you play forty-eight full minutes, it's not an official game.

The referees cleared the spectators off the court and resumed play. The Warriors tried to get the ball to Wilt again, but he didn't want it. He stood at midcourt, shaking his head, with a big smile on his face. He didn't want to score any more. Wilt knew very well that "a hundred points" sounded a lot better than "a hundred and two points."

The buzzer rang. The final score was 169–147.

"Okay, I think that should be enough time," Miss Z said as she fiddled with her computer.

She typed a few more commands on the keyboard and hit the Enter key. There was a brief buzzing sound, and then the screen on the Board lit up. The five bands of color appeared. After a few seconds they merged together to form one band of intense white light. Julia, Isabel, and Luke shielded their eyes but didn't dare look away.

The light seemed to stretch out and away from the surface of the Board until coming to a point about three feet in front of it. There was that humming sound, and then there was an image, almost like a hologram. It was flickering at first, and then it solidified.

David was back.

He fell to his knees, panting and gasping for breath. The others rushed over to him.

"Are you okay, dude?" Luke asked David, putting his beefy arm around him. "Where were you?"

"It works!" David replied. "It really works!"

CHAPTER 7

THE
FLASHBACK FOUR

THE OTHERS HELPED DAVID INTO A CHAIR. HIS hair was a little messed up, and his clothes were somewhat disheveled. But he had a wild look in his eyes, as if he had just stumbled off his first roller coaster ride and couldn't wait to go back for another one.

"It works!" he kept repeating. "I can't believe it works!"

Miss Z had a satisfied *I-told-you-so* look on her face.

"What was it like?" Isabel asked David. "Did it hurt? Was it scary? Was it fun? Tell us *everything*!"

"I was *there*," he said, "and Wilt Chamberlain was there. It wasn't like he was a hologram or I was in some kind of virtual reality simulator. I was right there, a few rows up from the court, watching the game. Wilt scored a hundred points, and I saw it happen. Everybody was going nuts. It's hard to describe what it felt like. It was scary, but it didn't hurt. It was *awesome*. I pinched myself to make sure it was real."

"I always thought time travel was impossible," Luke said, shaking his head. "That's what my teacher told us in science class. And she's an expert."

"I used to think that too, Luke," said Miss Z. "You know, before the Wright brothers got off the ground at Kitty Hawk in 1903, the experts thought human flight was impossible. It couldn't be done. But these two ordinary bicycle mechanics did it. Before a guy named Roger Bannister came along in 1954, the experts thought it was impossible for a human being to run a mile in less than four minutes. But he did it. And before I built the Board, the experts thought time travel was an impossibility. But I did it."

"Did you figure it out all by yourself?" asked Isabel.

"Oh no. I have a team of techs who helped me," she admitted. "I drove them hard to solve this problem. Worked them like dogs to finish as quickly as possible. And I paid them handsomely. But my firm—Pasture Company—owns the technology."

"Why do you call it Pasture Company?" asked Isabel.

"It's my little in-joke," replied Miss Z. "I can't take you to the future . . . but I can take you to the *past*ure."

David suddenly remembered the souvenir he had brought back with him from 1962. He took the rolled-up game program out of his back pocket and passed it around for the others to see.

"Check it out," he said. "See, it's even got the date on it."

"Did you find that on the ground at the Hershey Arena?" asked Miss Z.

"Nah, I made a bet with some kid that Wilt was going to score a hundred points," David told him. "I won, of course, so he had to give me his program."

David was pretty proud of himself, but Miss Z shook her head in disapproval.

"I don't know how I feel about that," she told David. "Taking artifacts from the past is risky business. You might remove some little thing that turns out to be important, and change the course of history."

"Sorry," David said. "I wasn't thinking about that."

Luke, Isabel, and Julia admired the program. They hadn't asked to see any physical proof that David had actually traveled through time, but now they had it.

"If I were you, I'd sell that thing on eBay," Julia told him. "I bet a lot of basketball fans would want the program from the only game in history when somebody scored a hundred points. It may be a one-of-a-kind. You could make a lot of money."

"Sell it?" David said, taking it back. "No way. I'm keeping it forever. Seeing Wilt score a hundred points was the most exciting moment of my life."

"See what I mean?" Miss Z told them. "That's exactly what I was telling you. I sent David back to see Wilt Chamberlain score a hundred points in a game. But I could have sent him *anywhere*, to *any* time. Imagine sitting in the boat next to George Washington as he crossed the Delaware River on Christmas Day in 1776. Imagine watching the Wright brothers taking off on their first flight at Kitty Hawk. Imagine seeing Michelangelo working on the ceiling of the Sistine Chapel or Leonardo da Vinci painting the *Mona Lisa*. The possibilities are *endless*! You four could work as a team."

The four kids, who had been skeptical and even dismissive of Miss Z earlier, were now convinced that she was the real deal. She had promised them the adventure of a lifetime, and she was obviously capable of delivering it.

Each of them was anxious to go on a trip, for

their own special reason. Isabel was thinking about her future. She was sure she wanted to go to college someday and study history, maybe to become a history teacher when she grew up. She imagined how awesome it would be to go back in time and witness history with her own eyes, and be able to tell her students about it one day. It would be the best research imaginable.

Luke didn't care much about history, but seeing the look on David's face when he came back made Luke want to experience the same kind of excitement. Lately he had come to admit to himself what his parents had been telling him for a long time—playing video games all the time is boring. Staring at a screen for hours on end is deadening. He was craving something in the real world that couldn't be duplicated in two dimensions.

Julia had a similar feeling. Shopping and buying things for yourself is always fun, of course, but there's something hollow about it. You reach a point where you have more than enough stuff, and getting even *more* of it doesn't bring you happiness. Your brain cries out for some other kind of fulfillment.

And David, well, after his experience going back to watch Wilt Chamberlain, he was ready for just about anything. It was like he'd just tasted ice cream for the first time. He wanted more.

"So what will *our* adventure be?" Isabel asked anxiously.

"Can I assume all four of you are on board?" asked Miss Z.

"Yeah!" they replied as a group.

"Good!" Miss Z said. "Before we get to your adventure, there's one more order of business. We need to give you a name."

"What do we need a name for?" asked David. "We already have names."

"I can't constantly be calling you David, Luke, Isabel, and Julia," said Miss Z. "You need a group name. Something punchy."

"How about the Time Team?" suggested Isabel. "Because we travel through time, and we're a team."

"That's lame," said Julia.

"How about the Awesome Avengers?" suggested Luke. "Because we're awesome, and we avenge stuff."

"Oh please," groaned Isabel.

"There are four of us," said David. "It could be the something Four. A word that begins with the letter *F*. Funny. Fearless. Fantastic."

"There's already a Fantastic Four," said Luke. "It

was a comic book and a movie."

"Furry," said David, thinking out loud. "Flying . . . forever . . . flashing. *Flashback!* How about the Flash-back Four?"

"That sounds cool," said Luke. "The Flashback Four."

"I like the sound of that," Miss Z said. "Ladies?"

"It works for me," replied Isabel.

"It's better than the Awesome Avengers," said Julia.

"Then it's agreed," said Miss Z as she took some papers out of her desk drawer. "From now on you are the Flashback Four."

"So where are we going?" asked Isabel.

"You're going home, for now," Miss Z replied, handing each of them a sheet. "Get a good night's rest, and get these permission slips signed by a parent. I'll see you here right after school lets out tomorrow."

CHAPTER 8

THE ADVENTURE
OF A LIFETIME

I KNOW WHAT YOU'RE THINKING, READER. NO
parent in their right mind would give permission to
let their son or daughter get zapped through time by
some experimental smartboard and sent on a mysterious "field trip" to who-knows-where.

That's true. But the next day, precisely at three
thirty, all four members of the Flashback Four
returned to the Hancock Tower with their permission
slips signed and dated.

To get his parents to agree, Luke told them his
class would be taking a tour of Fenway Park, and he
needed permission. As a diehard Sox fan, his father

signed the form without hesitation. He never looked at it to see what he was signing.

David, on the other hand, was totally honest with his parents. He simply said, "Some rich white lady invented this magical smartboard and she wants to send me and some other kids back in time with it."

"Very funny," his mother replied, taking the permission slip and signing it. She never read the form either.

Isabel had a long conversation with her parents, who were still learning English. She explained that she needed their permission to go on an educational field trip that could very possibly help her get into college and help her career someday. As soon as he heard the word *college,* Isabel's father was reaching for a pen.

Julia's parents were both out of the country on separate business trips, so she couldn't ask them to sign the permission slip. She just signed it herself, forging her mother's signature, as she had done many times before when her parents weren't around.

When the Flashback Four arrived together on the twenty-third floor, Mrs. Vader took their permission slips and ushered them into the office. Miss Z was not there yet.

"The boss is running a bit late," Mrs. Vader told

the kids. "Can I offer you some tea and cookies while you're waiting?"

"That would be lovely," Isabel said, using her best manners.

Mrs. Vader wheeled in a cart and poured a cup for each of them.

"Do you know where Miss Z is going to send us?" Julia asked.

"I have no idea."

"Have you been on one of these trips yourself?" asked Isabel.

"Oh, goodness no," replied Mrs. Vader. "I'm just Miss Zandergoth's secretary."

"Do you mind my asking what happened to her?" Luke asked.

"I believe she's stuck in traffic," said Mrs. Vader.

"No, I mean, why is she in a wheelchair?"

"It's . . . rather personal," Mrs. Vader replied, after thinking it over for a moment. "I'd rather not get into it."

Isabel noticed that Mrs. Vader's eyes suddenly appeared watery. A single tear slid onto her cheek, and she quickly wiped it away with her sleeve.

"Does she have a disease or something?" asked David.

Mrs. Vader just nodded her head and replied simply, "ALS."

"That's Lou Gehrig's disease," Luke said. "My uncle had it. Amyotrophic lateral sclerosis. There's no cure. My uncle died like a year after he got the bad news."

"Is Miss Z going to die?" asked Isabel.

"I've said too much already," Mrs. Vader replied, wheeling the cart out of the room.

There was an awkward silence as Luke, Julia, Isabel, and David thought about what they had just heard, and wondered if Miss Z's illness was the reason why they had been recruited in the first place.

"I bet that's why she was in such a big rush to finish building the Board," Luke commented.

At that moment, the door opened and Miss Z rolled into the room.

"Sorry I'm late!" she said cheerfully. "Are you kids excited?"

"Yeah!" all four replied.

"Exactly where and when are we going?" asked Luke.

"Well," said Miss Z, "when I say 'Four score and seven years ago,' what does that mean to you?"

"The score of a ball game?" asked David.

"Are you kidding me?" Miss Z said, rolling her eyes.

"Don't they teach you kids *anything* in social studies these days?"

"Four score and seven years ago has something to do with the Gettysburg Address," Isabel said.

"Right," Miss Z replied. "And what do you know about the Gettysburg Address?"

"Not much," Isabel admitted. "I think I was absent the day we studied that."

"Wasn't the Gettysburg Address where Abraham Lincoln lived in Gettysburg?" asked Julia.

"No!" Miss Z shouted, slapping her forehead. "Lincoln never lived in Gettysburg!"

"Then why did he have a Gettysburg address?" Julia asked.

Luke rolled his eyes. "The Gettysburg Address was a speech he gave, in Gettysburg," he said quietly.

"*Thank* you!" said Miss Z.

She rolled closer so she could more easily command their attention.

"July first, 1863," she said. "The Battle of Gettysburg was the turning point of the Civil War, and its bloodiest battle. Fifty *thousand* casualties. Do you know how many men that is? Imagine Fenway Park filled to capacity. Now add another thirteen thousand soldiers."

"Wow," David said.

"Four months later, President Lincoln came to the battlefield to dedicate the cemetery where many of those soldiers were buried," Miss Z continued. "That's when he delivered the Gettysburg Address. It's probably the most famous speech in American history."

"So you're going to send us there?" asked David.

"Yes," Miss Z replied. "I'm going to send you to Gettysburg, Pennsylvania, on November 19, 1863."

"What for? So we can *see* it?" Julia asked. "Do you need us to be eyewitnesses or something?"

"In a way, yes," replied Miss Z. "Actually, I have a job for you to do there."

"Aha, here's the catch," David said. "It's about time, right? I knew there would be a catch."

Miss Z rolled over to her office wall filled with photos depicting great moments in history.

"I have been accumulating these pictures my entire adult life," she said, sighing.

Then she pointed to the one spot on the wall that was empty.

"See that space? My goal is to fill it. I need a picture of Abraham Lincoln delivering the Gettysburg Address. And I need *you* kids to shoot that picture."

FOUR SCORE AND SEVEN YEARS AGO

READER, I KNOW WHAT YOU'RE THINKING. THERE are plenty of photos of Abraham Lincoln. You've probably seen lots of them. In fact, the Library of Congress has about 7,000 photos taken during the Civil War, and 130 of them show Lincoln. There's just one problem. Read on.

"Now, let me get this straight," Luke said to Miss Z. "Your plan is to send the four of us to Gettysburg, Pennsylvania, in the year 1863 so we can take a picture of Abraham Lincoln giving the Gettysburg Address. Do I have that right?"

"Exactly!" Miss Z replied. "You see, Luke,

photography is a form of time travel, when you think about it. We snap a picture and we capture that moment in time. Forever. It becomes ours. With that photo, we bring the past to us. It could be a hundred years in the past, or five minutes. Either way, we get to step inside that memory. A photo allows *all* of us to travel through time."

"I don't get it," Isabel said. "Why do you need another picture of Abraham Lincoln?"

"You must understand that photography was a very young art form in Lincoln's time," Miss Z told the group. "The first photograph in history was taken in 1826, when Lincoln was a teenager. Pictures were still a novelty during the Civil War. The average person didn't own a camera. They were very big, expensive, and hard to use."

Miss Z rolled herself over to her desk and took a folder out of one of the drawers. The children gathered around to peer over her shoulder.

"Look at this," she said, opening the folder. "There are only *three* existing photographs taken at Gettysburg on November 19, 1863. None of them are close-ups, and none of them show Lincoln actually giving the speech. This is one of the photos."

"It's blurry," Julia commented. "Which one of those guys is Abraham Lincoln?"

Miss Z took a magnifying glass out of her drawer and moved it slowly across the sea of faces in the wide crowd shot.

"It's the guy on horseback," Luke said. "See? He's wearing one of those stovepipe hats. And it looks like he's saluting the troops. It must be the president."

"That's what everybody thought for a long time," Miss Z said. "But if you blow this photo up really big, you'll see that the guy on horseback has longer hair than Lincoln, and his beard is fuller. Lincoln's beard was kind of wispy, and he had a slight gap between his beard and his sideburns. This guy doesn't have that."

"It's the stovepipe hat that throws you off," David noted. "There are a bunch of guys in the picture wearing those hats."

"Also, the guy on the horse has epaulets on his shoulders," Miss Z told them. "We know that Lincoln was wearing a plain black overcoat that day. And by the way, presidents didn't start saluting the troops until Ronald Reagan did it in 1981."

"So who's the guy with the stovepipe hat?" asked Julia.

"He's probably just some local official," replied Miss Z.

"Then where's Abraham Lincoln?" asked Isabel.

"Over *here*," Miss Z said, moving the magnifying glass slightly to the left of the man with the hat. "He was in front of the speaker's stand, about to climb up onto the stage."

"It's hard to see that," said Luke.

"Yes, that's the problem," Miss Z said. "In any case, all the pictures are fuzzy and none of them shows Lincoln actually delivering the Gettysburg Address. And if we don't have a photo of an event, it's almost like the event didn't happen."

"If I go to a party and I don't shoot a selfie with my friends," Julia said, "I kinda feel like I wasn't even at the party."

The others rolled their eyes.

"Sometimes I feel like stuff we learn about in history is made up," Luke noted. "It doesn't seem real. Like Christopher Columbus arriving in America. Did that ever really happen?"

"Yes, but if you saw a photo of Columbus landing on the beach, you'd believe it, right?" asked Miss Z. "A photo brings a moment of time into our consciousness."

"Sometimes even *that's* not enough," Isabel said. "This girl I know told me she thinks we never landed on the moon. She says all those pictures of the astronauts are fakes. She thinks the whole space program was a hoax."

"That's ridiculous!" said Luke.

"I have a question," Isabel said. "If there were photographers at Gettysburg taking pictures, how come none of them got a shot of Lincoln giving his speech?

He was the president of the United States. You'd think the photographers would be all over him."

"Good question," Miss Z said. "Here's my guess—the Gettysburg Address is just ten sentences long. It only lasted about two minutes. By the time the photographers set up their primitive cameras with those big glass plate negatives, the speech was over. *That's* why I need to send you kids back to Gettysburg—to get the shot that those photographers missed."

"I can use my cell phone," Julia said, pulling it out of her purse. "Hey, maybe Abraham Lincoln will pose for a selfie with me! That would be cool to post on Instagram!"

Miss Z snorted.

"Cell phone?" she said, opening up another drawer on her desk. "No, if you're going to go back to 1863, you're going to do it *right*."

She reached into her drawer and pulled out a very expensive Nikon digital single-lens reflex camera with a zoom lens.

"Nice," Luke said, examining the camera closely. "And you're gonna show us how to use this thing? It looks pretty complicated."

"Of course."

"So I guess you're gonna sell the picture we take

and make millions of dollars from it, eh?" asked Julia.

"Is that all you think about, money?" asked Isabel.

"No," Julia replied, shooting an angry look at Isabel.

"I'm not going to sell it at *all*," Miss Z said. "I already told you—I want to put the photo up on my wall. And eventually, down the line, I hope to build a museum filled with these photos of great moments in history. But of course, that won't be for a long time."

The Flashback Four shot nervous glances at one another. They knew that Miss Z would probably not be around to see the opening of her museum. But Miss Z didn't know they knew that.

During the discussion about Gettysburg, David had been sitting and listening without saying much, but looking increasingly uncomfortable.

"I've got a problem with all this," he finally announced.

"What is it, David?" asked Miss Z.

"Well, in case you haven't noticed, my skin is a little darker than everybody else's here," he said pointedly. "And you're planning to send the four of us back to 1863."

"Yeah, so?" asked Julia, not quite putting two and two together.

"There was this little thing called *slavery* going on

back then," David told them. "You may have heard of it. If I go back to 1863, they might try to make me into a slave."

"Gettysburg is in Pennsylvania," Luke pointed out. "It was a Northern state. They didn't have slavery there."

"So what?" David said, his voice rising a bit. "I saw that movie *Twelve Years a Slave*. The guy was in New York when he got kidnapped. I'm not about to get myself sold into slavery just so we can take a picture."

All eyes turned to Miss Z.

"I'm glad you brought that issue up, David," she said. "You know, it was no coincidence that Martin Luther King Jr. delivered his 'I Have a Dream' speech in front of the Lincoln Memorial. The Gettysburg Address is engraved on the wall there. Here, let me show you something."

She opened the middle drawer of her desk and fished around until she found a faded, yellowed piece of paper.

"Lincoln was wrong about one thing," Miss Z told the group. "In the Gettysburg Address, he wrote, 'The world will little note, nor long remember what we say here.' As it turned out, what he said there would be remembered for a long time."

"Wow," Isabel said, putting out a hand to touch the paper. "Is that the real thing?"

"Oh, I wish it was," Miss Z said, chuckling. "There are only five known drafts of the Gettysburg Address in Lincoln's handwriting. This is just a copy. But I've studied it, analyzed it. Do any of you know what 'four score and seven years ago' refers to?"

David, Isabel, and Julia shook their heads.

"One score means twenty," Luke finally said. "So four score is eighty. Four score and seven years ago means eighty-seven years ago."

"That's right!" Miss Z said. "And do you know what year was eighty-seven years before 1863?"

Julia pulled out her cell phone. The others did the math in their heads. David came up with the answer first.

"Seventeen seventy-six," he said.

"Correct," said Miss Z. "When Lincoln wrote 'our fathers brought forth on this continent a new nation,' he wasn't talking about 1787, the year the Constitution was written and the United States became a country. He was talking about 1776, the year Thomas Jefferson wrote the Declaration of Independence."

"Your point?" asked Luke.

"There's a big difference between the Declaration

and the Constitution," Miss Z explained. "The Declaration said *all men are created equal*. The Constitution didn't say all men were created equal. In the Constitution, some men were more equal than others. Slavery was considered a part of life, in at least some parts of the country. The Constitution left it up to each state to decide on slavery. In fact, in the Constitution, a slave was counted as three-fifths of a person. At the time, one out of every eight Americans was a slave."

"So in the Gettysburg Address, Lincoln was talking about 1776, when we declared our independence from England," said Isabel.

"So in the Gettysburg Address, he was sort of hitting the Reset button on America, right?" asked Luke.

"Exactly!" said Miss Z. "It was almost like we became born again as a nation. That's why those ten sentences are so important."

"Why do you need four of us?" he asked next. "Obviously, only one of us is going to take the picture."

"I want to take it!" David shouted.

"I want to take it!" Isabel shouted.

"I want to take it!" Julia shouted.

"I need *all* of you to go," Miss Z told them, "and I need you to work as a team. The Civil War was still going on in 1863, remember. This could be dangerous.

You may encounter trouble along the way. You'll need to work together and watch each other's backs. I know the four of you can. That's why I chose you. You're the Flashback Four."

David, Luke, Julia, and Isabel nodded. In the last hour they had gone from being four disinterested seventh graders to being a team with a mission to accomplish.

"We'll be witnessing history," Isabel said quietly. "And making it, too."

"That's right," Miss Z agreed, rolling herself over to look at the lone empty space on the wall once again. "History is like a big jigsaw puzzle, with some of the pieces missing. Every so often, we're lucky enough to stumble upon one of those pieces and figure out what happened in that time period. The Board will just make it a little easier to find those pieces."

David got up from his chair and went over to the Board.

"Let's do this thing," he said.

GO BOIL YOUR SHIRT, BY JINGO!

ONE BY ONE, LUKE, ISABEL, AND JULIA GOT UP
and joined David at the Board.

"Let's go," David said, clapping his hands together.
"Zap us back to the good old days, Miss Z. We'll take
that picture for you. No worries."

Miss Z sighed and chuckled to herself.

"Not so fast," she told the group. "First you kids
need to do some preparation."

"I'm prepared," Luke said. "I'm ready to go right
now."

"You're prepared?" asked Miss Z. "How do you
think the people of Gettysburg are going to react in

1863 when *you* suddenly show up on the street wearing a Boston Red Sox T-shirt?"

"They'll think I'm *awesome*!" Luke said, slapping a high five with David. "Because the Sox are awesome."

"Please avoid using the word *awesome* unless you're referring to Niagara Falls, or the Grand Canyon, or something that's *truly* awesome," Miss Z told Luke. "I've got news for you. The Red Sox don't exist in 1863. And for that matter, neither do T-shirts."

"What difference does it make?" David asked. "Aren't we just going to show up, take the picture of Lincoln giving the speech, and blow out of there? They'll barely even notice us."

"If everything goes perfectly, yes," Miss Z explained. "But things may not go perfectly. This may not be easy. You may encounter obstacles. I didn't invest millions of dollars into this technology to get the simple stuff wrong."

The kids sat back down in their chairs. Miss Z instructed them to take out their cell phones and text their parents that they would be a little late for dinner.

"First we need to talk about language," she said. "The kind of English spoken in 1863 is not the same as the English we speak today."

"How was it different?" Isabel asked.

"Every era has its own words and expressions," Miss Z told her. "For instance, instead of saying 'thank you,' a person in 1863 was more likely to say 'much obliged.' Instead of saying they 'want' something, they might say they have a 'hankering' for it. Do you see what I mean?"

"Like, 'Ah gotta mosey on down the road a piece,'" Luke said in an exaggerated accent. "Or, 'Ah gotta skedaddle before mah corn bread burns.'"

"Something like that," said Miss Z. "You'd better light outta here lickety split, old chum, and I don't wanna hear none of your bellyaching and balderdash."

"So you're saying that we're supposed to talk funny?" David asked.

"To the people you're going to meet, the four of you talk funny right *now*," Miss Z told him. "Believe me, if somebody from 1863 came to our time and listened to any of us talk, they would think it was *hilarious*."

Miss Z rolled over to her desk and took out some sheets of paper from a drawer. She handed one to each of the kids. The title at the top of each page was CIVIL WAR SLANG, and a list of vocabulary words was printed underneath.

"Memorize these words and expressions," she instructed. "It's important."

The kids studied the sheet, and it wasn't long before they were poking fun and cracking wise.

"Hey, if you want to tell somebody to get out of here," said Julia, "you're supposed to say, 'Go boil your shirt!'"

Everybody laughed.

"If you're angry, you're supposed to say, 'I'm fit to be tied!'" said Isabel. "Or 'You get my dander up.'"

"What's dander?" asked David. "Isn't that the stuff that cats have in their fur?"

"It doesn't matter what it is," Miss Z told him. "Just *say* it. And for goodness' sake, don't use any curse words in 1863! If you need to curse, say 'by jingo' or 'land sakes.'"

"Hey, you know what the quickstep is?" asked Luke. "That's when you have diarrhea!"

Everybody laughed again.

"If that don't beat all!" said Luke.

"See? You're getting the hang of it," Miss Z told them. "In 1863, people don't think, they *reckon*. They're not tired, they're *tuckered out*. They don't go over there, they go over *yonder*. They don't pat their stomach, they *slap their pappy*."

"Slap their pappy?" All four cackled loudly.

"Oh, keep your britches on," Miss Z told them. "If

you kids go in there talking like it's the twenty-first century or peacocking about in a Red Sox shirt, you're going to stand out like a sore thumb. People won't know what to think. They might tar and feather you, or run you out of town on a rail."

"Do we have to memorize this whole sheet?" asked Julia.

"Yes," said Miss Z. "Or, as they would say in the 1860s, the whole kit and caboodle. Does anybody have any other questions?"

"This is like school," David complained.

"That's not a question," Miss Z replied. "And yes, it is a little bit like school. It's called *learning*. I promised you the adventure of a lifetime. I never said it was going to be an *easy* adventure. Now let's talk about food."

"Food?" asked David. "Why do we have to worry about food? It's not like we're staying overnight."

"What if something goes wrong?" Miss Z said. "You might have to wait hours for Lincoln to deliver his speech. You're going to get hungry."

"So we'll go to McDonald's," Julia said, throwing up her hands. "What's the big deal?"

Luke rolled his eyes and used all his powers of restraint not to tell Julia that she was an idiot.

"They didn't have McDonald's in 1863," Miss Z explained patiently. "There was no fast food. No Doritos. No candy bars. And they didn't have Whole Foods or Trader Joe's either. There were no supermarkets at all."

"How did they survive?" Julia asked.

"Most people lived on farms or in rural areas," said Miss Z. "So they grew their own food. Or they hunted, traded, foraged, or fished. A lot of the foods we eat today simply didn't exist back in the 1860s."

"So what did they eat?" asked Isabel.

"All kinds of things," replied Miss Z. "Frizzled beef. Baked goose. Succotash. Plum pudding . . ."

"Ugh, gross," Julia groaned.

". . . Oyster pie. Calves' feet. Oxtail soup. Stewed kidney. Boiled turtle . . ."

"No wonder people died in their thirties back then," said David.

"Actually, I think they ate much *healthier* back then," said Miss Z as she punched the button on her intercom. "Mrs. Vader, it's time for our snack."

A few seconds later, the office door opened and Mrs. Vader came in holding another platter full of some sort of unidentifiable food.

"Here, taste this," Miss Z told the kids.

"What is it?" asked Luke hesitantly.

"Just taste it."

"I'm not tasting it until you tell me what it is," Luke said.

"If I tell you what it is, you won't taste it," Miss Z replied.

Nobody was reaching for the platter. The girls looked disgusted.

"Okay, *I'll* taste it," David finally volunteered.

"You are a brave young man, David," said Mrs. Vader as she handed him a small piece of bread with some kind of meat on top of it. He put it in his mouth. Luke picked up a piece and did the same.

"It tastes like chicken," Luke announced.

"Mmm, not bad," said David. "What is it?"

"It's mutton," said Mrs. Vader.

David gagged, and spit into a napkin.

"Gross!" he said. "I'm not eating mutton. What's mutton, anyway?"

"Mutton is sheep," Luke told him, as he finished his piece.

"Ewww, gross!" exclaimed both of the girls.

"I'm not eating a sheep!" said David.

"Why not?" asked Miss Z. "You eat cow. You eat chicken. Why not eat sheep?"

"Sheep are *cute*," said Julia.

"Pigs are cute," Mrs. Vader said. "Do you eat ham, or bacon?"

"Y'know, this stuff isn't bad," Luke said, taking another piece from the platter. "They should sell a McMutton sandwich at McDonald's."

"You are totally gross," said Julia.

"I'm a vegetarian anyway," Isabel said. "I won't eat anything that has a face."

"What about pumpkin?" asked David. "Pumpkins have faces."

"Did they have any gluten-free food in the 1860s?" asked Isabel. "I'm thinking of cutting out gluten."

"Are you kidding me?" asked Miss Z. "No, they didn't have gluten-free food. And there was no Coke or Pepsi. No protein bars. No Happy Meals. They didn't have any packaged, processed junk. They ate real *food*. And if you ask for chicken fingers, don't be surprised if they actually cut the fingers off chickens and serve them to you."

"Okay, now you are *totally* grossing me out," said Julia.

"Chickens have fingers?" asked David.

"Just be prepared for unusual foods, okay?" said Miss Z. "Now we're running out of time. We need to talk about your clothing. Or, as they would say back in 1863, your duds."

"Red Sox! Red Sox!" chanted Luke as he stood up to show off his T-shirt again.

"You want to blend in with the crowd, Luke," Miss Z explained. "You want to look like everyone else. Mrs. Vader?"

Mrs. Vader took the platter of mutton away, and then came back into the office rolling a long rack of antique clothing.

"Oh, fun!" said Julia. "We get to play dress up!"

The rack was actually filled with men's clothes—or, more specifically, *boys'* clothes—from the 1860s. Julia and Isabel jumped up excitedly and began going through the trousers, jackets, and shirts. The boys were less than enthusiastic.

"You gotta be joking," Luke said. "Do we really have to wear that stuff?"

"If you want to fit in, yes," said Miss Z.

After some mixing and matching, discussing and debating, the girls chose outfits that would look good on Luke and David. For Luke, that meant wide-legged dark woolen knickers, a white shirt with a ruffled collar, a paisley vest, and a frock coat trimmed with braid and buttons.

For David, it was a navy blue waistcoat with gold buttons over a checkered vest; a white button-down, cuffed shirt; and a black tie. Isabel picked out light blue trousers and a gold-buckled belt for David. Julia added a jaunty military-style cap to top things off.

"Go ahead, boys," Miss Z told them. "Try 'em on."

Luke and David groaned as they followed Mrs. Vader out of the office. She opened the men's bathroom for them. A few minutes later they emerged in costume. Luke looked particularly uncomfortable and a bit sheepish.

"Oh my," Julia said flirtatiously. "Ah must say, you boys look mighty handsome in those new duds."

"Land sakes! Ah think Ah may just faint dead away," said Isabel.

Both girls were giggling, making exaggerated curtsies, and fanning themselves with imaginary fans.

"I look like a big doofus," Luke said.

"No you don't," David told him. "In 1863, this is what the *cool* guys wore. I don't know about you, but I'm looking *good*."

"Hey, you're lucky," Miss Z said. "Some young men wore kilts in those days."

"That's just *not* gonna happen," said Luke.

Mrs. Vader rolled the rack of boys' clothes out of

the office and came back in pushing an even longer rack full of clothes for girls. Isabel and Julia swooned at the sight of them.

"They're so *beautiful*," Isabel said. "Where did you *get* all this stuff?"

"From a costume shop," Miss Z replied as she pulled a poplin dinner dress with linen collar and cuffs from the rack. "The sewing machine became widely used in 1846. That made it much easier and faster for dressmakers to create these wonderful designs."

Julia picked out a blue petticoat trimmed with crimped frills and lace and held it up in front of her. Isabel chose a taffeta walking dress edged with quilling of satin ribbon. Almost instantly, the girls abandoned those choices in favor of a velvet cloak lined with silk and a simple frock trimmed with ostrich feathers. Then there were decisions to be made regarding velvet ribbons, ornamental roses, medallions, sashes, and bows.

"I can't decide if I should go with the embroidered French cambric or the pleated trim of braid and wide-scalloped lace," said Julia. "Can I try them both on?"

"Of course!" said Miss Z.

The boys groaned again.

When the girls left the room to try on the clothes,

David and Luke discussed the Red Sox's chances in the next season. After what seemed to be an eternity—but was just a few minutes—the girls returned in their new finery. Both of them had chosen dresses that puffed out dramatically as they reached the floor, like two enormous church bells. Julia was now wearing a straw bonnet with a lace demi-veil. Isabel had accessorized her outfit with a fan, white gloves, and a parasol. The girls spun around dramatically, so the boys could get the full effect.

"Lovely! Gorgeous!" said Miss Z and Mrs. Vader, clapping their hands. David and Luke did their best to not look impressed.

"Well, how do you like our outfits, fellas?" asked Julia.

"It looks like you could hide a small army under there," David commented.

"It's not very practical," said Luke. "What if you have to run wearing that thing?"

"A *lady* does not run," Julia informed him haughtily. "The boys will run to *me*."

"I just *love* these shoes," said Isabel. "Can I keep them after we get back?"

"Sorry," said Miss Z. "I have to return them to the costume shop."

"Can we get out of here now?" Luke finally asked. "By the time we get to 1863, the war will be over."

"The war won't end for another two years," Miss Z informed them. "But it's late now. I've given you a lot to learn and think about. For now, I want you four to get out of those duds, go home, and get a good night's sleep. Tomorrow, after school, you leave for 1863."

CHAPTER 11

GOING TO GETTYSBURG

AS SOON AS SCHOOL LET OUT THE NEXT DAY, David, Julia, Isabel, and Luke rushed to the John Hancock Tower. They met as a group in the lobby and took the elevator up to the office of Pasture Company. Mrs. Vader buzzed them in and ushered them into the office.

"Well, the Flashback Four are here!" Miss Z said when she saw them. "I'm glad you all decided to come back. I was afraid that one or two of you might chicken out on me."

"No way," David said. "I am pumped."

"How about the rest of you?" asked Miss Z. "Pumped?"

"Pumped!" said Luke. "Let's go!"

"Majorly pumped," said Isabel.

"Minorly pumped," said Julia. "I was wondering, why did you choose *kids* to do this job? Why didn't you hire some grown-ups to do it?"

"Kids have certain advantages over grown-ups," Miss Z explained. "You're smaller and faster, for one thing, so if you get into trouble, you can escape more easily. You think on your feet better than adults. You're not so set in your ways, so if you have to switch gears in the middle of something, you can handle it. But most of all, I chose you because you're not legal adults. When adults mess up, they get in trouble. They can be punished. They can be put in jail."

"We can get away with doing crazy stuff," Luke said. "Because we're too dumb to know better."

"I wouldn't put it in those words," said Miss Z. "But essentially, yes."

"It sounds like you're expecting us to have problems," Isabel said.

"I wouldn't have gotten to where I am today if I didn't expect the unexpected," said Miss Z. "You should, too. That reminds me, before you change into your costumes, there are a few last-minute things we need to go over. What I'm about to tell you is *very* important, so listen carefully. When you get to Gettysburg, you'll be in 1863. It's going to seem almost like a different world. There will be no cell phones, no computers—"

"We know, we *know*," Luke said wearily. "No cars, no planes, no television, no nothing. We've heard it all before."

"In fact, I'd like you to give me your cell phones to hold," said Miss Z.

Isabel, David, and Luke put their cell phones on the desk. Julia recoiled in horror.

"My cell phone?" she asked. "I feel like it's . . . almost a part of me."

"You won't be able to use it where you're going," Miss Z explained, "and if I'm holding it, you don't have to worry about losing it."

Reluctantly, Julia put her cell phone on the desk.

"Good," said Miss Z. "Now, you need to be aware of one quirk about the Board. My team is still working on this technology. Right now, it can only send you to a particular time and place *once*. So I can't be shuttling you back and forth between Boston and Gettysburg every five minutes because you forgot something or whatever. We need to do this once, do it right, and bring you back here safely."

"So in other words, we can't mess up," said Isabel.

"There's no margin for error."

"Exactly. Now, look at this."

In the middle of her desk, Miss Z had a simple map of Gettysburg, Pennsylvania, that she had drawn. The four kids gathered around to examine it.

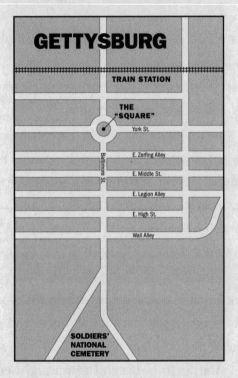

"Where are we going to land?" Luke asked.

"Most likely, right *here*," Miss Z replied, jabbing her finger at a large circle in the middle of the map. "This is the center of town. It *still* is, in fact. In 1863, they called it the diamond, but today it's called Lincoln Square. It's a circle, but they call it a square. Go figure. Anyway, Baltimore Street starts right there, going south, and the biggest buildings in town surround it. You won't be able to miss it."

"Is that where Lincoln will be giving the address?" asked David.

"No," Miss Z said. "Remember, he's coming to Gettysburg to dedicate a cemetery for Union soldiers who died in the battle. That cemetery is at the edge of the village, a short walk down Baltimore Street. It's called Soldiers' National Cemetery, right *here*."

Miss Z slid her finger down Baltimore Street to show the kids exactly where they would need to go.

"Looks like less than a mile," Luke commented. "It must be a really small town."

"It is," said Miss Z. "There's going to be a big military parade that will start at the square and end at the cemetery. You'll be able to follow the crowd to get to the cemetery."

"How do you know exactly what's going to happen?" asked Luke.

"It's called *research*," Miss Z replied. "Now, this next part is crucial. I know from doing my research that Lincoln will be delivering the Gettysburg Address at around two o'clock in the afternoon. So after you take the photo, I need you to walk back up Baltimore Street to the square, where you first landed. At three o'clock *sharp*, you need to be standing in the middle of the square. That should give you plenty of time. Then I'll activate the Board to scoop you up and bring you back here safely."

"Got it," said Isabel, making a mental note. "Three o'clock."

"*Be* there," Miss Z said seriously, folding up the map and handing it to Luke. "Right after the speech is over. It's important."

"What happens if we aren't back at the square at three o'clock?" asked David.

"Let's just say you could be stuck in 1863 for a *long* time," Miss Z said pointedly. "Now, which one of you has experience with a camera? Julia, you're always talking about shooting selfies. Do you think you can handle this responsibility?"

"Sure!" Julia replied excitedly.

"This is a *real* camera," Miss Z said, carefully taking the Nikon out of her drawer.

"Uh, that looks complicated," Julia said, backing away from the camera.

"My dad has a fancy camera," Luke said. "I've fooled around with it a little."

Miss Z handed Luke the Nikon. Miss Z took a few minutes to explain how to focus and how to adjust the shutter speed and aperture settings. The Nikon had a powerful zoom lens, but she instructed Luke to try and get as close to Lincoln as possible. Photos come out sharper and clearer when you don't use the zoom.

She told Luke it was a very expensive camera and advised him to keep it out of sight until the moment he was ready to take the picture. Most people in 1863 had never seen *any* camera before, much less a high-tech digital one from the future.

The Nikon wasn't hard to use, but there were a lot of buttons on it and the controls could be a little confusing. Luke took some practice shots of Julia, David, and Isabel to get the hang of it.

"Remember, you are *only* going to Gettysburg to take this photo," Miss Z said, addressing all four of the kids. "That is your sole purpose. You're not going there to make friends, to sightsee, or to bring back souvenirs. Do not disturb history in any way. You take pictures, not things. Do you understand?"

All four heads nodded.

"And I need you to stay together as a group at all times," Miss Z continued. "That's why I recruited you. Work as a team. Don't go running off and getting into trouble."

"Okay, can we go now?" asked Julia impatiently.

"One last thing," said Miss Z as she reached into her desk drawer once again. She pulled out a small black box, slightly smaller than a cell phone. "Isabel, I'm putting you in charge of this."

"It looks like a little cell phone," she said.

"How come *she* gets the cell phone?" complained Julia. "I want the cell phone."

"It's *not* a cell phone," said Miss Z. "Needless to say, an ordinary cell phone would be useless in 1863."

"Then what is it?" asked David.

"I call it a TTT. That stands for Text Through Time."

"Text Through Time?" asked Luke. "You mean to say we'll be able to send texts back and forth with you while we're in 1863?"

"Correct."

"Cool!" said David.

"Wait a minute," Isabel said. "Doesn't texting use satellites just like cell phones do? There were no satellites in 1863. How can this thing possibly work?"

"Isabel," Miss Z said, putting a hand on the girl's

shoulder. "I spent a billion dollars to create this technology. It *works*. Twenty years from now, *everybody* will have one of these. Time travel is going to be as commonplace as Skyping is today. You'll be able to swap texts with relatives who died centuries ago. Instead of going to Disney World, people will be going back in time on vacations. It will be a whole new industry. Believe me. This is the future. It's inevitable."

"If you say so," Isabel said, examining the buttons on the TTT.

"I need you to keep me informed about where you are and what you're doing," Miss Z told her. "When you arrive at the square, text me right away. Give me updates. And be careful with this thing. It's the only one I have. In fact, it's the only one in the world."

"You can count on me," Isabel said.

"Also, when you arrive in Gettysburg, be respectful," Miss Z told the Flashback Four. "The mood is likely to be somber. Remember, thousands of people were wounded or died there just four months earlier. Some of their loved ones will probably be there. In my research, I've found that people can grieve for up to four to six months after things like this."

"So no cracking jokes and stuff," said David. "Okay, we get it."

"Good. Mrs. Vader! Let's get these kids ready."

Mrs. Vader came into the office and led the Flashback Four to the restrooms to change their clothes. Luke and David came out first, looking very sharp in their knickers and waistcoats. They stood awkwardly in front of the Board, waiting for the girls to come out. Five minutes later the girls appeared, smiling, twirling around, and doing their best not to step on their enormous dresses.

Isabel slipped the TTT into a pocket that had been specially sewn into her dress. The four kids took their places in front of the Board. It was a tight squeeze, mainly because Isabel and Julia's dresses took up so much space. They had to stand boy-girl-boy-girl to fit in.

"Tighter," Miss Z instructed, as if she was taking a group photo. "Get closer together. You don't want me to cut somebody's arms off, do you?"

The kids jammed together until Miss Z was satisfied that they all fit within the frame of the Board. She turned on the power and then rolled over to her computer.

"Are you all ready?" she asked. "Last chance to change your mind."

"Nobody's backing out," Luke said, holding the camera tightly. "Do it."

"I'm scared," Isabel said.

"It will be fine," David assured her. "It will all be over in a few seconds."

"What do we do if something goes wrong?" asked Julia.

"Text me. I'll try to help," Miss Z said. "But it may be up to you. That's why there are four of you. Figure out a solution. Be strong."

"Bye-bye!" said Mrs. Vader. "Good luck! Have fun!"

Miss Z typed some commands on her computer, took one last look, and hit the Enter key. The Board buzzed for a few seconds and then lit up. The five bands of color appeared, and then merged into one band of intense white light. It was like staring at the sun.

"It's blinding me!" said Julia, squinting and shielding her face.

"Close your eyes," David told her. "Hold on!"

"I feel something happening," Luke reported. "It's like I'm melting."

"That's normal," Miss Z assured him. "It means you're about to go back."

The humming sound started, and the kids grabbed each other's hands for support. The white light was flickering now, first slowly, and then faster, like a fluorescent bulb that was partially burned out. Something was clicking on and off.

"I don't—" was the last thing anybody said.

And then they vanished.

CHAPTER 12

THE SQUARE

DAVID HIT THE GROUND RUNNING. ISABEL AND Luke crashed into each other and nearly fell down. Julia almost landed on a stray cat. But fortunately, nobody on the street seemed to notice when these four strange kids from another century suddenly appeared in the middle of the square.

A large wooden building in front of them was decorated with red, white, and blue bunting, and topped with a sign. . . .

GETTYSBURG HOTEL. BUILT IN 1797.

"The Board works!" Isabel said breathlessly.

"I *told* you it worked," said David.

"In the back of my mind I thought that the whole thing was just a trick," Luke said. "I figured we were part of some crazy reality TV show."

"We're in *Gettysburg*," Isabel marveled. "And this isn't the twenty-first century, that's for sure. This is like watching a documentary on TV, but we're right in the middle of it. This is so cool!"

Just so you know, reader, Gettysburg was founded in 1761 by an innkeeper named Samuel Gettys. It's located in central Pennsylvania, close to the Maryland border and about sixty miles from Baltimore. If you look at it on a map, you'll see that ten roads converge at Gettysburg, which is a big reason why the Union and Confederate armies chose to pick a fight with each other there.

Still getting over their disbelief, the kids turned to look around the square. There was a high, wooden flagpole right in the middle, its flag featuring just thirty-five stars. Wooden and redbrick buildings surrounded the square. None of them were higher than four stories, because elevators had only been invented a few years earlier.

The road that circled the square wasn't paved. It

was made of dirt. There were no cars on it, of course, but plenty of horses. Even though Gettysburg was not in the western part of the country, the kids were reminded of Western movies they had seen.

Miss Z had cautioned them to be respectful because the atmosphere in Gettysburg would be somber, but it was just the opposite. The square was jammed with men, women, and children, and it looked like a big celebration. People were shouting, chanting, and waving little American flags. A military band was playing on one side of the square, and a college glee club was singing "When Johnny Comes Marching Home" on the other. In the middle were smaller groups of roving serenaders. A little girl rolled a wooden hoop down the street, pushing it forward with a stick. An old man weaved around, greeting friends and strangers he encountered. He was clearly drunk. There was merriment in the air. Everybody seemed to be having a good time.

People were dressed much like Luke, Isabel, Julia, and David. Some were decked out in their best finery, while others seemed to be wearing rags. Everybody—men and women, boys and girls—wore some kind of a hat. Many of the men sported stovepipe hats like the one made famous by Abraham Lincoln.

David looked around for suspicious men who might possibly be slave traders. Luke checked to make sure the camera had made the trip safely. He thought about taking a few pictures of the square, but decided to wait for the Gettysburg Address. If the battery were to die before Lincoln started to speak, there would be no way to recharge it. Isabel checked to see if she still had the TTT. Everything was in order. The Flashback Four started walking around the square.

"What is that smell?" Julia suddenly asked, wrinkling up her nose.

"I think it's horse manure," David replied.

"Oh, gross!"

"Well, what did you expect?" asked Luke. "They've got a lot of horses here. Horses produce a lot of manure."

"I expected clean, fresh air," Julia replied. "Isn't 1863 before they had pollution? Isn't this before they started digging coal and oil out of the ground and burning it? The air should smell *wonderful*."

"They burn *wood*," Luke told her. "That causes a lot of pollution, too."

"It would smell a lot better if you'd watch where you were walking," David told Julia. "Look at your shoe."

Julia looked down. Then she screamed.

"I stepped in it!" she shouted, horrified. "Oh, I think I'm gonna throw up!"

"Will you be cool?" Luke told Julia, putting his hand over her mouth. "You're drawing attention to us. People around here probably step in horse manure all the time. It's no big deal to them."

"So that means I should *like* it?" Julia said disgustedly. "Ugh, these shoes are totally ruined! And we just got here!"

"Look, you need to calm down," Isabel told her. "This is not a problem. Give me the shoes."

"Gladly!"

Isabel took the shoes and rubbed them in the dirt to clean them off the best that she could. She scraped them up pretty badly, but at least she got the manure off them. Julia put the shoes back on gingerly, still disgusted and complaining.

"I just thought it would be cleaner in 1863," she said. "Everything looks so dirty."

"You've seen too many movies," Luke told her. "I bet a lot of the houses here don't even have running water. People probably bathe once a week, if that. Can you imagine how tough it is to clean one of those dresses? They probably wash 'em once a year."

Julia was still adjusting her shoes when a couple

of teenage boys walked by, whistling "Yankee Doodle."

"Good day, ladies!" one of the boys said with a smile. "Lovely day to be out for a walk." The other one tipped his hat and smiled as he passed. Julia and Isabel responded by collapsing into giggles.

"I think those boys were flirting with us!" Isabel whispered.

"The one on the left was kind of cute," Julia said.

"Don't flatter yourself," David told her. "They were just being friendly."

"I notice they weren't being friendly to *you* guys," Julia replied. "They were just being friendly to *us*."

"Who cares who they were being friendly to?" asked Luke. "We have a job to do. Remember, we're supposed to text Miss Z to let her know we got here safely. She told us to do that before anything else."

"Do we really need to tell her every little thing we do?" asked Julia. "It's not like she's our mom or anything."

"I think you're forgetting something," Isabel said. "Miss Z has that disease, remember? We don't know how long she has to live. Getting that picture may be the one thing that keeps her going. The one thing that makes her want to get up in the morning."

"Besides, she promised the adventure of a lifetime,"

David said, "and look around—here it is! We're gonna see Abraham Lincoln give the Gettysburg Address! Think about that for a minute! We're gonna see one of the most important events in history, in real time. Nobody ever did this before."

"Okay, okay!" Julia said. "Go ahead and text her."

Isabel took out the TTT and started tapping the buttons.

"Hey, hide that thing!" David told her. "If the people here see you using it, they're gonna totally freak out."

"Shhhhh!" Luke told David. "Keep your voice down, dude! If the people hear you say 'freak out,' they're gonna freak out."

"Don't say 'dude,' dude!" David told Luke. "Nobody said 'dude' in 1863."

Isabel turned her back to the square so people would not be able to see what she was doing. She switched on the TTT and tapped out . . .

WE R HERE. SAFE & SOUND

"No way that thing's gonna work," Julia said to nobody in particular. "It's impossible to text through time."

As each second passed with no response, Julia appeared to be more and more correct. And then, after about fifteen seconds . . .

Bzzz.

This appeared on the screen . . .

SPLENDID! WHERE R U EXACTLY?

Isabel just about dropped the TTT when she saw the words come through.

"It works!" she said.

THE SQUARE, Isabel tapped out. LINCOLN SQUARE.

A few more seconds passed. *Bzzz.* And then . . .

EXCELLENT. PROCEED TO THE CEMETERY.

David pulled out the map Miss Z had given them, then turned around. There were no signs, so it was hard to tell which of the roads branching off the square was Baltimore Street. A man with a cane was walking by, so David approached him.

"Excuse me, good sir," he said, trying to sound as grown up as possible. "My friends and I are green-horns around these parts. Would you be so kind as to direct us to Baltimore Street?"

"Down thataway," the man replied. "Where ya headed?"

"We're fixin' to see President Lincoln deliver his Gettysburg Address."

"His *what*?" asked the man.

"I mean . . . uh . . ."

Luke pulled David aside.

"They didn't call it the Gettysburg Address before he delivered it, you dope!" he whispered. "It's like they didn't call it World War I during that war because nobody knew there was gonna be a World War II."

"I'm terribly sorry," David said to the man. "What I meant to say was that my friends and I got a hankering to see the president speak."

"You folks are a mite early," the man replied. "Old Abe ain't gonna be dedicating that cemetery 'til tomorrow."

"Tomorrow?" Isabel asked, flabbergasted. "Isn't today November nineteenth?"

"Nope," the man told her before continuing on his way. "I reckon it's the eighteenth. All day, in fact."

The Flashback Four turned to one another.

"What are we doing here *today*?" Luke asked.

"Miss Z must have messed up," Julia said. "She sent us a day early."

Isabel grabbed for the TTT.

U SENT US 2 THE WRONG DAY!!! she typed.

There was a long silence. And then . . . *Bzzz*.

IT WAS A TYPO. I HIT THE 8 INSTEAD OF THE 9. SORRY.

"A typo?!" Luke said angrily. "The lady invested billions of dollars in this technology. She made sure we all had the right clothes. She told us how we're supposed to talk. She drew us a map. She took care of every detail. And then she types the *date* wrong?"

Isabel typed furiously . . .

BRING US BACK HOME! SEND US HERE TOMORROW.

Bzzz. This time the response came back quickly . . .

NO CAN DO. THE BOARD CAN ONLY SEND YOU 2 A TIME PERIOD ONCE. I'M SORRY. DEAL WITH IT.

"Deal with it?" David said. "Is she kidding?"

"Mistakes happen, I guess," said Isabel. "She told us we should expect the unexpected. Well, this sure is unexpected."

"Oh great," Luke said, thinking out loud. "This means we'll have to find a place to sleep here tonight. We'll have to get some food. I didn't bring a toothbrush. Did you guys? And where are we going to shower? We'll have to—"

"Relax," David said, putting a hand on Luke's shoulder. "We can handle this."

"Hey, you know what? I don't care," Julia said, a smile spreading across her face. This just means we have more time to spend here. It's going to be *fun*! Let's go exploring!"

Julia started skipping away in the direction of Baltimore Street.

"We need to stay together," Luke shouted after her. "Miss Z told us—"

"Oh, lighten up, will you?" Julia shouted back. "We're not babies."

The others had no choice but to follow Julia as she skipped down the street, giggling and chatting with every passerby.

"Hello, m'lady!" Julia said to a woman pushing a baby carriage. "Isn't it a simply lovely day? Isn't 1863 a simply lovely time to be alive?"

"Julia!" David shouted. "Knock it off!"

Julia continued her frolic around the square, and then stopped suddenly. Two men in Union army uniforms were standing near the corner, on crutches. Each of them was missing one leg, and one of them was also missing an arm. Clearly, they had lost their limbs fighting in the war. And they were the *lucky* ones, Julia realized. Thousands of their fellow soldiers were buried in the cemetery that President Lincoln would be dedicating.

Julia looked around. For the first time, she noticed the signs of war in Gettysburg. Picket fences and walls of buildings were riddled with bullet holes. Windows were shattered and had not been replaced. Sad-eyed women were holding pictures of their husbands who had died in battle. It wasn't all a party.

"I'm sorry," Julia said to the group. "I wasn't thinking."

"Forget it," David said. "It's all good."

There was the blast of a train whistle. It was the Conewago, a twenty-five-ton steam locomotive coming in from the nearby town of Hanover Junction. It pulled into the Gettysburg train station a block away, and more people streamed out of it into the square.

The population of Gettysburg was only 2,400, but there were already 15,000 people in town, with more arriving all the time. Every hotel was booked solid. Every bed was taken. It didn't seem like the little town could hold any more people. The square was getting more crowded. It was becoming hard to stay together as a group.

"Hey, y'know, I bet President Lincoln is already here," Luke said.

"What makes you say that?" Isabel asked.

"Well, it's not like they have Air Force One," Luke replied. "Lincoln probably came from Washington, DC, by train, and it must take hours with these old trains. So he most likely had to come in the day before his speech, right?"

"Maybe we can meet him," said Isabel.

"That would be cool," David said.

"Where do you think we would find him?" asked Luke.

"Beats me."

While this discussion was going on, it suddenly occurred to Luke that Julia was not with them.

"Where's Julia?" he asked, looking around.

"I don't know," said Isabel. "I thought she was with you."

"Why should she be with *me*?" Luke asked. "I thought she was with *you*."

"Don't look at *me*," David said, putting his hands in the air. "I don't know where she is."

Julia was gone.

CHAPTER 13

PRIVATE PROPERTY

DAVID, LUKE, AND ISABEL WERE IN A PANIC. THEY whirled around frantically, trying to take in the whole square at once. Julia was nowhere to be seen.

"Where *is* she?" Luke asked urgently.

"She was here a minute ago," said David.

"I *knew* this was a mistake," Isabel said. "What are we gonna do if we can't find her?"

It seemed like one thing after another was going wrong. First the Flashback Four were sent to Gettysburg on the wrong day, and now one of them had run off. What if Julia was lost? The others would have to leave without her. Worse, what if she was kidnapped?

Isabel wondered if it could have been those two boys who were flirting with them. Or it might have been the man they had asked about Baltimore Street. It could have been *anybody*. There were hundreds of people milling around the square, and some of them looked pretty shady.

"We need to text Miss Z," Isabel said.

"What's *she* gonna do?" David asked. "She can't help us. We have to find her on our own."

"Let's not panic," Luke told them. "I'm sure she's right nearby. She couldn't have gone very far. Be positive."

The three of them scanned the sea of faces scattered across the square. Just about all the women were wearing those big, bell-shaped dresses, just like Julia.

"If we were in our regular clothes, we would be able to find her right away," David said. "She would stand out."

At that moment, the TTT buzzed in Isabel's pocket.

"Oh man, what does Miss Z want *now*?" she muttered, pulling the device out. This was on the screen . . .

WHAT IS GOING ON?

"Just ignore it," Luke advised Isabel. "We can deal with her after we find Julia. David, why don't you run over and check out *that* corner of the square? I'll check out the far corner. And Isabel—"

"Are you sure it's a good idea for us to split up?" Isabel asked. "I'm afraid we might—"

"Look! Over there!" David suddenly shouted, pointing at a house across the street. "Is that her?"

"I don't see anything," Luke said.

"A girl went in the door of that house," David told him. "It looked a little like Julia."

"*Everybody* here looks a little like Julia," Luke pointed out.

"Was she with anybody?" asked Isabel.

"I don't think so," David said. "But somebody might have been in front of her. Let's go!"

They hustled through the square, dodging people left and right as they made their way across the street.

"Maybe Julia just had to go to the bathroom," Isabel said hopefully, elbowing her way around an elderly couple.

"She would have said something to one of us," David said.

The house they were running toward was a three-story redbrick building, one of the tallest in Gettysburg. A plain-looking house, it didn't have any fancy carvings or flourishes on the outside walls, like

the bank on the other side of the square did.

Isabel, Luke, and David didn't know it yet, but I'll tell you, reader. This house belonged to David Wills, a thirty-three-year-old lawyer and a prominent citizen of the town. It was Wills who led the drive to create a cemetery honoring the Union soldiers who'd died in the Battle of Gettysburg. He acquired the site of the cemetery, arranged the design, planned the ceremony, and invited President Lincoln to come and give a speech at the dedication. During the battle itself, Wills led people up on the roof of this building to watch the fighting in progress.

David pulled open the front door. Isabel and Luke peeked inside. Nobody was there. They entered the house.

"Nice place," David whispered as they tiptoed

through the dining room and into the living room. "Whoever lives here must be rich. They have a fireplace in every room."

"That doesn't mean they're rich," Luke whispered back. "That means they didn't have any other way to heat the house."

"Shhhh! Quiet!" Isabel said.

Actually, Wills *was* quite wealthy. All the rooms were elegantly decorated with expensive mahogany cabinets, flowery wallpaper, and gas lamps along the walls. The place looked like a museum.

Isabel, Luke, and David stopped for a moment to listen. There were footsteps above.

"Come on, she must have gone upstairs," Luke told the others.

"We shouldn't be in here. This is private property," Isabel whispered as they climbed the steps. "We could get in trouble."

"What if somebody lured Julia up there?" David whispered back. "We can't just do nothing."

"We could get shot for trespassing!" Isabel said. "They shoot people for stuff like that in 1863."

"I have news for you," David informed her. "They shoot people for stuff like that in *our* time too."

"Shhhhh!"

At the top of the stairs, they looked left and right. There were several bedrooms on the second floor. All the doors were open, except for one.

"In here," whispered Luke, his hand on the doorknob.

Isabel held her breath as Luke pulled open the bedroom door. And there, standing beside a small oval table, was Julia. She was alone.

"Julia!" the three shouted, catching her by surprise.

The bedroom was ornate, like the ones downstairs. Paisley carpet. Fancy fireplace with an oil painting on the wall above it. There was a rocking chair in the corner by the window, which looked out on the square. The red curtains were pulled aside, revealing white lace underneath.

"What are you doing in here, Julia?" Isabel asked. "We were supposed to stay together as a group."

Julia had a guilty look on her face. She pushed the door closed behind them.

"I . . . uh . . . had to go to the bathroom," she whispered.

"This isn't a bathroom," David said, pointing out the obvious.

Julia was holding some pieces of paper in her hand. When she realized the others were staring at them, she hid them behind her back.

"What's that?" Isabel asked.

"It's nothing."

"If it's nothing, let us see it," David insisted, holding out his hand.

Julia sighed, and then handed over the papers. David looked at them and gasped.

"It's . . . the Gettysburg Address!" he said, his voice going up in pitch.

"Are you *serious*?" Luke asked, taking the pages. "Lemme see that."

There were three white pages, about six by nine inches. The first two were filled with steady, even handwriting. The third page had just a few lines on it. Some of the words had been crossed out and replaced with others, but the first line was unmistakable—*Four score and seven years ago . . .*

"It *is* the Gettysburg Address!" Luke said.

"This must be the room where Lincoln is sleeping tonight!" Isabel said, looking around. There was a familiar-looking stovepipe hat on a dresser in the corner.

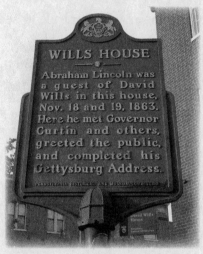

"Wait a minute," Luke said, turning to face Julia. "Were you trying to *steal* the Gettysburg Address?"

Julia hung her head, refusing to make eye contact.

"Don't tell Miss Z," she begged. "Please?"

At that moment, the TTT buzzed in Isabel's pocket again. She showed the others the words on the screen . . .

REPEAT. WHAT IS GOING ON?

"Don't tell her!" Julia said.

Isabel tapped out this response . . .

WE R DEALING WITH IT. LIKE U SAID.

Luke, David, and Isabel turned back to face Julia.

"Are you *crazy*?" David asked her. "Did you really think you would get away with this?"

"I . . . I don't know," Julia replied. "It seemed like a good idea at the time."

"I remember learning in school that Lincoln wrote the Gettysburg Address on the back of an envelope," Isabel recalled. "How can *this* be the Gettysburg Address?"

"That whole envelope thing is a myth," Julia told her. "The truth is that he started writing the speech in Washington, before he left for Gettysburg. He finished it right here, in this room. Or, he's *going* to finish it here, later tonight."

"How do *you* know what he's gonna do?" Luke asked. "How did you even know to come to here?"

"There's this thing called research," Julia replied. "I looked it up online the night before we left. I found out that a lawyer named David Wills invited Lincoln to stay in his house the one night he would be in Gettysburg. This is his house. That's when I got the idea to come here, if I had the chance."

"But why would you want to steal the Gettysburg Address?" Isabel asked.

"Remember what Miss Z told us?" Julia said, lowering her voice. "There are only five known copies of the speech in Lincoln's handwriting. That's *it*. Do you have any idea of how much money a rough draft of the Gettysburg Address would be worth? *Millions!*"

"So what?" Isabel said. "It's stealing. It's wrong."

"You're not poor, y'know," David told Julia. "You go to that ritzy private school, don't you? Your parents are probably loaded. Why would you steal *anything*, much less this?"

"Do you have any idea of how dangerous this is?" Luke asked Julia.

"Maybe that's why I did it," she admitted.

"You would never be able to sell the Gettysburg Address anyway," Isabel pointed out. "It would be like stealing the *Mona Lisa* and trying to sell it to somebody. It's too famous."

"How do *you* know?" Julia asked. "I bet there's a collector out there who would give just about *anything* for a previously unknown rough draft of the Gettysburg Address in Lincoln's handwriting."

"She's probably right," David said.

"Hey, if it's money you're after, I have a better idea," Luke told Julia, putting the papers back on the little table. "But we gotta get out of here now. President Lincoln is still working on this. If you take it, he won't be able to deliver his speech tomorrow. We're under strict orders not to change history, remember?"

"Let's go," Isabel said. "Somebody could walk in here at any moment."

"Relax," Julia said. "Everybody's out on the square partying."

"Oh yeah?" said Luke. "What happens if the Secret Service walks in here right now? We'd all go to jail."

"They don't *have* a Secret Service in 1863," Julia told him. "I looked that up, too. They started the Secret Service *after* Lincoln was assassinated."

"Well, what happens if Lincoln *himself* walks in here right now?" Luke asked.

"That would be cool," David said. "I would thank him for the Emancipation Proclamation."

"What's that?" Julia asked, prompting a group eye-roll from the others.

Before the kids left, they couldn't resist taking one last look around the room where Lincoln would be sleeping that night. The bed itself was a beautiful Rococo revival style with a white bedspread and a mahogany headboard carved with florals and scrolls. There were four pillows on it. On the bedside table was a jug of water. On the wall was a fancy mirror in a scalloped wooden frame.

"Hey, what's that thing under the bed?" David asked, peering down.

"It's a chamber pot," Luke told him. "You pee in it."

"They peed in *pots*?" David asked, dumbfounded.

"What, you think they had toilets inside the house in the old days?" Luke told him. "They had a privy outside. But nobody wants to go outside to pee in the middle of the night. Especially in the winter. So they used a chamber pot."

"You're telling me that the president of the United States had to pee in a *pot*?" asked David.

"Where *else* is he gonna pee?" Luke asked.

"I don't know," David replied. "Maybe he peed out the window."

"Are you out of your mind?" Luke asked. "*Nobody* does that!"

"I did it once," David admitted.

"Gross!" said Julia.

"Will you two quit arguing?" whispered Isabel. "Is that footsteps? I think somebody's coming!"

In fact, somebody *was* coming. The Flashback Four

looked around frantically for places to hide.

"Oh no!" Isabel said. "I *told* you we should get out of here!"

"It might be the president!" said Julia.

"Quick!" David said. "Hide under the bed!"

"What, all four of us?" Isabel asked. "There's no room!"

"Okay, David and I will get under the bed," Luke instructed. "You two hide in the closet."

"There *is* no closet!" Isabel whispered frantically.

At that moment, the door was flung open. A very angry-looking young man entered the room.

And he was holding a gun.

CHAPTER 14

ANOTHER LINCOLN

NONE OF THE FLASHBACK FOUR HAD EVER HAD A gun pointed at them before. It is a terrifying thing. The group let out a collective gasp and instinctively stepped back in horror.

"Don't shoot!" Julia shouted, throwing her hands in the air. "We didn't do anything!"

The boy standing before them couldn't have been more than ten years old. His dark hair was parted neatly on one side, framing a boyish face. He had a smirking smile, which revealed a set of extremely crooked teeth.

He was wearing a full Union army uniform,

complete with a sword attached to his belt. To the Flashback Four, the boy was obviously too young to be a soldier. But then again, they couldn't be completely sure. Maybe when things got desperate during the Civil War, children were recruited to fight for their country.

Luke, David, and Isabel followed Julia's lead and put their hands in the air. The boy pointed his gun at each of them without saying a word.

"Please put that down," Isabel said, trying to sound calm. "Let's talk this over."

Still the boy hadn't spoken, and that made the Flashback Four even more frightened. As the only African American in the group, David was thinking that if any of them was going to get shot, it would probably be him. Luke was thinking that if the kid brought them to the authorities, they might never get back to the twenty-first century. Julia was thinking what her chances of survival would be if she simply made a run for it. Would he really shoot a girl? Isabel was thinking that ever since they arrived in Gettysburg, one thing after another had gone wrong.

"Let's just give him what he wants," Isabel said, without taking her eyes off the boy. "Don't try to be a hero."

"Maybe he doesn't speak English," said Julia. "How will we even *know* what he wants?"

With those big, fluffy dresses, the girls were in no position to run, fight, or do much of anything to resist. But Luke and David shot a glance at each other, both knowing what the other was thinking—*We could take this kid.* They were older and bigger than the boy, and they had him outnumbered two to one. Of course, the kid had a gun in his hand. But it was just a little pistol. It probably only had one bullet in it. He wouldn't be able to shoot *all* of them.

"Look!" David barked suddenly, pointing to his left. "Out the window!"

It was the oldest trick in the book, of course. But then, maybe the book hadn't been written yet in 1863. That was what David was counting on, anyway.

Fortunately, the distraction worked. The boy glanced to his left for a moment, and in that moment Luke and David jumped him. Luke kicked the kid's wrist, causing him to drop the gun. It clattered to the wooden floor.

"Land sakes! You hurt me!" the boy shouted. "What in tarnation did you do *that* for? I'm going to tell my papa on you!"

Luke and David pinned him to the floor and sat on him to make sure he couldn't get free. He didn't resist. He looked like he was going to cry.

Isabel quickly scooped up the gun before the boy could get it again.

"It's not real," she said, examining it. "It's a toy pistol."

Luke and David helped the boy to his feet.

"You shouldn't be pointing a gun at people," scolded Luke. "Even if it's a toy. Somebody might shoot *you*."

Isabel gave the boy his toy back.

"I was just havin' a little fun," he said, wiping the

tears off his face with his sleeve.

It was hard to understand what he was saying. The boy had a severe speech impediment.

"Who *are* you?" Luke asked him. "What's your name?"

"Tad," the boy replied.

Luke didn't quite understand.

"Ted?" he asked.

"Not Ted. *Tad*."

It was still hard to understand him.

"Did you say Thad?" Isabel asked.

"Not Thad. *Tad*!"

It was still hard to figure out what the boy was trying to say. He was clearly frustrated over his inability to communicate.

"I'm Tad! T-A-D, *Tad*," he said. "Didn't you ever hear of me? I'm *famous*. I'm Tad Lincoln!"

It took a moment for that information to sink in.

"You mean, you're Tad Lincoln as in *Lincoln* Lincoln?" asked Julia.

"You're . . . President Lincoln's *son*?" asked David.

"Yes!" he said, nodding his head and rubbing his arm, which already had a bruise on it. "He is my papa."

It was true, reader. Thomas "Tad" Lincoln was the fourth and youngest son of Abraham and Mary Todd

Lincoln. It was the president who nicknamed him Tad because he had a large head and a small, squirmy body that reminded him of a tadpole.

Tad's speech problems were a result of being born with a cleft palate, which is an opening that develops when the bones of the skull don't completely join together. Nowadays it can be treated with surgery, but back in the 1860s there wasn't much that could be done to help people with cleft palates.

"Sorry we roughed you up there, Tad," David said, brushing dust off the boy and smiling at him. Now that they knew who the boy was, all four of them were acting overly friendly toward him. That's all they'd need, to have the president's son tell his father that they had beaten him up.

"Your gun looked real at first," Luke told him.

"It *is* real," Tad replied. "Papa gave it to me for my birthday in July. I turned ten years old."

Besides the speech impediment, there seemed to be something definitely *different* about Tad Lincoln. He didn't act like an average ten-year-old.

"Why are you here, Tad?" Isabel asked.

"Why are *you* here?" Tad replied. "This is Papa's room, not yours."

The kid had a point. But they weren't about to tell

him that Julia had snuck up to the president's room specifically to steal the Gettysburg Address.

"We . . . uh . . . umm," Julia sputtered.

"I could have the four of you arrested and thrown in jail, you know," Tad told them. "That's what happened to Jack."

"Jack? Who's Jack?" asked David.

"He is my soldier doll," Tad replied, the smirky smile returning to his face. "He is a bad boy. One time I caught him sleeping at his post, so I held a court-martial. And another time he was spying for the enemy, so I charged him with treason."

"Jack is a . . . doll?" asked Julia.

"Yes, and a very naughty boy," Tad said. "I sentenced him to be shot at sunrise. Me and my brother Willie buried him in the rose garden at the White House. But Papa gave him a pardon, so we had to dig him up again. Papa is always pardoning people."

Tad seemed to enjoy telling the story, and he clearly liked the attention he was getting. While he was talking about his soldier doll, the Flashback Four shot furtive glances at one another. Tad seemed to have calmed down, but nobody wanted to say anything that might set him off.

"Do you go to school, Tad?" asked Isabel.

"Heck no!" the boy replied. "School? Why should I waste time learning how to spell and all that when there are so many fun things to do?"

"But you *must* go to school," Julia told him. "Doesn't everybody have to go to school?"

"I have tutors," Tad replied. "But they don't last very long. If they try to teach me reading and writing and such, I make Papa get rid of them."

"You don't know how to read or write?" asked David.

"Heck no," Tad said. "Don't need to. My papa is the president. When he is finished, he says we'll move back to Illinois and I'll have people read and write *for* me."

The four glanced at one another again. None of them was about to tell Tad that shortly after his father's second inauguration, he would be cut down by an assassin's bullet.

"Do you want to play with me?" Tad suddenly blurted out. "We could play army out on the battle-field."

"That sounds like a lot of fun," Isabel said diplomatically, "but we have important stuff we need to do."

"Like what?" Tad asked.

"Oh, you wouldn't believe us if we told you," David said.

"Betcha I *would*."

The Flashback Four looked at one another once again. Luke put his arm around Tad's shoulder.

"Well, Tad, the truth is that we come from the twenty-first century," he told the boy. "We traveled through time so we can take a picture of your father tomorrow while he's making his speech at the cemetery."

"I believe you," Tad said, as if what Luke had told him sounded completely logical.

Tad noticed Luke's camera for the first time and asked if he could see it. Luke showed it to him, being careful not to let the boy touch it.

"I like that toy," Tad said. "Can I have it?"

"Oh, no, I'm sorry," Luke told him. "It's not a toy. We need this to take the picture. It's very important."

Tad's face went from glad to sad in an instant. It looked like he was going to start crying again, or possibly throw a fit. He wasn't used to people telling him he couldn't have whatever he wanted. You don't say no to the president's son.

"If you don't give that toy to me," Tad said, losing control, "I will scream!"

"I really wish I could, Tad, but—"

Tad started screaming. Luke quickly clapped a

hand over the boy's mouth. Tad tried to bite it.

"Tad, listen to me," Luke told him, putting the boy in a headlock. "I'll tell you what I'll do. Tomorrow, after your father's speech, you meet me right back here and I'll give you a toy. How does that sound?"

Luke was totally lying, but it seemed to calm Tad down somewhat. Luke released him from the headlock.

"Usually when I ask people for toys, they give them to me," Tad said.

"Not this time," Luke told him. "Sorry."

"Where is your father right now, Tad?" Isabel asked. She figured that maybe if she changed the subject, Tad would forget about the camera. And that's exactly what happened.

"Papa is visiting Mr. Seward," Tad said.

"Mr. Seward" was William H. Seward, who served as the governor of New York and was a United States senator before becoming Lincoln's secretary of state. He had taken the train to Gettysburg with the president and was staying in a hotel nearby.

"We saw your father's speech on the table over there," Julia said. "Is he going to finish writing it tonight?"

"I dunno," Tad replied. "He gives lots of speeches. Do you want to meet Papa and ask him yourself?"

"That would be awesome!" David said, and when Tad looked at him oddly, he amended it to, "That would be great! Can you arrange that?"

"You have to pay me," Tad told them.

"*Pay* you to meet your father?" Julia asked. "How much?"

"A nickel."

It seemed like a good deal.

"So if we give you a nickel, you'll introduce us to your father?" Isabel asked. She was already fishing around in her pocket for change. But the only thing in there was the TTT.

"I'll tell you what," David said. "I'll give you five dollars."

"Five *dollars*?" Tad said. "I only asked for five pennies."

"I don't have any change," David said.

"Okay," Tad said. "I'll take your five dollars."

"You drive a hard bargain, Tad," said Luke, laughing.

"Where did *you* get five dollars?" Isabel asked as David dug through his pockets.

"Remember those five-dollar bills Miss Z gave us?" David said. "Well, I brought one of them with me just in case I needed it. Pretty smart, huh?"

David finally found the bill in his pants pocket and

handed it over to Tad. The boy only looked at it for a moment or two before he started shouting.

"You trying to hornswoggle me? That's Papa's face!" he yelled, ripping the fiver into little pieces. "Papa's not on the five-dollar bill! This is a counterfeit!"

Tad started screaming again and throwing a fit.

"Guards! Guards!" he shouted. "Seize them! They are flimflam artists! Enemies of the state! They must be shot at sunrise and buried in the rose garden!"

"The kid is nuts!" yelled David. "Let's get outta here!"

CHAPTER 15

YOU CAN'T PLEASE EVERYBODY

"GO! GO! GO!"

Luke, David, Isabel, and Julia sprinted out of the bedroom and down the stairs of the Wills house as if the place was on fire. The girls were doing their best not to trip over their long dresses. Nobody was bothering to look back to see if Tad Lincoln was chasing them. All they wanted to do was get away from him. Only when they made it out the front door and around the busy corner did the Flashback Four stop to catch their breath.

"Did we lose him?" Luke asked, turning around and gasping for breath.

"I think so," David said, leaning over, his hands on his knees. "He's not gonna bother us."

"I just have to say," Isabel told them, "you guys were incredible up there! You looked like Batman and Robin."

"I can't believe you attacked Abraham Lincoln's kid!" Julia said, giggling uncontrollably.

"I've never even been in a fight before," Luke admitted.

"You were great," David told him. "I like the way you kicked that toy out of his hand. Do you do karate? Jujitsu?"

"No, man," Luke replied. "I just reacted. Dude, we make a good team."

"Hey, I'm sorry about that whole Gettysburg Address thing, you guys," Julia told the group. "I . . . don't know what I was thinking."

"Everybody makes mistakes," Isabel said. "Don't worry about it."

The sun was setting, and it was starting to get dark out on the street. The square was still teeming with people, and some of them were holding torches or small gas lamps to light up the night. A military band struck up a marching tune, and it was so loud that it was hard to hear the person standing next to you. The happy drunks on the street were a little more drunk than they had been earlier, and there seemed to be more of them. It was like there was a big block party going on, which made it easy for the kids to blend into the crowd.

Bzzz. Isabel felt a familiar buzzing in her pocket, and she pulled out the TTT. There was a new text from Miss Z . . .

WHAT IS HAPPENING?

Isabel showed it to the others.

"We better not tell her about our little . . . meeting with Tad Lincoln," Luke said. "She might freak out."

"Thank you!" Julia said.

"Just tell her nothing exciting is going on and that everything's fine," David suggested.

Isabel tapped out words to that effect on the TTT and waited to see if she would get a reply. It took a few seconds. *Bzzz.*

DID YOU FIND A PLACE TO SLEEP? asked Miss Z.

NOT YET, Isabel typed back, disguising the fact that they hadn't even started looking for a place to sleep yet.

Bzzz.

GET SOMETHING TO EAT AND A GOOD NIGHT'S REST, Miss Z texted.

TAKE PHOTO TOMORROW. LET ME KNOW IF ANYTHING UNUSUAL HAPPENS.

ROGER, Isabel typed back.

"Who's Roger?" Julia asked.

"Roger means yes," Isabel told her. "It means I understand the message."

"Didn't you ever see any old war movies?" asked Luke. "Guys in the military say Roger all the time."

"Why don't they just say yes?" asked Julia. "Yes is easier to type than Roger."

"Who cares about that?" David said. "I'm beat. We gotta find a place to sleep or I'm gonna fall over."

"We'd better look for a hotel," Julia suggested.

"Forget about *that* idea," David said.

As you might imagine, reader, finding a hotel was out of the question. Gettysburg was a very small town, with just a few hotels. Every room had long been filled, and many of them were overstuffed with four or more people. Even if the kids had been able to find a hotel room, they had no way to pay for it. Not knowing they would be spending the night, Miss Z didn't think it was necessary to get them any 1863 money. The only one who'd brought cash was Luke, and Tad Lincoln had just torn up his five-dollar bill. No, they would have to find a place to stay for free.

"We should get something to eat before we look for

someplace to stay," Isabel suggested.

"Yeah, I'm starving," David said. "Too bad there's no McDonald's around here."

"We might have to kill an animal and eat it," Luke pointed out. "That's what they did in the old days before supermarkets."

"Gross," Julia said. "I'm not killing an animal."

"Oh, but it's okay if somebody *else* kills it for you?" asked Luke.

"Sure," Julia replied. "I'm so hungry, I'd eat mutton right now."

None of the kids had noticed, but a crowd had started to gather around the corner, right outside the Wills house. People were whispering to one another and pointing up. Julia, Luke, David, and Isabel went over there to see what all the excitement was about.

"What's going on?" Isabel asked a gray-haired lady with a bun in her hair.

"They say Old Abe is inside this house," the lady said. "Somebody spied him up in that window."

Everyone in the crowd was peering up at the window on the second floor.

"He must have come back to the room right after we left," David whispered to Luke. "I bet they snuck him in the back door, to avoid the crowd."

"Old Abe! Old Abe! Old Abe!"

People on the street had begun a slow chant, hoping that the president might come out and say a few words. More people joined in the chant, and quickly there were hundreds of voices.

"Old Abe! Old Abe!"

Suddenly, the white lace curtain was drawn back and a face appeared in the window.

"Look! It's *him*!" somebody shouted.

It was the unmistakable face of Abraham Lincoln, the face that the Flashback Four had seen on TV, in photos, on classroom walls, five-dollar bills, and pennies. He looked very much the same. It was a kindly face with a somewhat dark complexion. Isabel got goose pimples when she saw him.

"I can't believe I'm seeing him in person," Isabel whispered. "Look at him!"

"Hurrah for Old Abe!" a man shouted, and he let out a *whoop* as he took the hat off his head and threw it in the air.

People were cheering, whistling, and pointing. Some had tears of joy in their eyes, or simply gaped at the president, open-mouthed. He waved to the crowd and smiled as he bowed his head slightly to acknowledge their attention.

It was hard for Luke and his friends to appreciate what seeing Lincoln in person meant to the people surrounding them on all sides. There was no CNN, or round-the-clock news in those days. No TV, radio, or internet. Most people would *never* get the chance to see a president—or *any* famous person—in the flesh. This was a once-in-a-lifetime opportunity.

"He's more handsome than he looks in the pictures," said one lady in the crowd.

"God bless our president!" several people shouted.

"God bless America!"

Lincoln continued waving to the crowd below him on the street. As he did, Luke's attention was distracted by the man standing beside him. He had his hands in his pockets and a sneer on his face. The guy looked familiar somehow, but Luke couldn't remember where he might have seen him before.

"Scum of the earth," the man muttered under his breath disgustedly. "Look at that buffoon, soaking in his adulation."

The man had a slight southern accent. Luke turned to get a better look at him. He was a handsome man, with brown, piercing eyes and dark, curly hair that piled mostly on top of his head. Neatly trimmed mustache. He was wearing a fine wool suit and a thick tie. Very well put together. Clearly, he wasn't just some crazy person out ranting on the street. Luke knew he'd seen the man's face before—or perhaps a photo of him—but he couldn't recall where. He elbowed David in the side.

"Ever seen that guy?" he whispered.

"Nope," David replied.

The man continued muttering, while staring daggers at Lincoln.

"Tyrant," he said. "That uppity, no-'count, mealy-mouthed blowhard."

Then he spat on the ground as the president continued waving to the crowd.

"Can't please everybody, I guess," Luke whispered.

The lace curtain fell back in the window, and as quickly as he had appeared, the president was gone. End of show. The crowd let out a groan. They had only witnessed a brief glimpse of Abraham Lincoln. For some people, that would be enough. They would be able to tell their grandchildren that they had seen the president of the United States with their own eyes.

The crowd was beginning to disperse when the front door of the Wills house suddenly opened, and none other than Lincoln himself came out on the steps. He had put on his familiar stovepipe hat, and it made him look even taller than his usual six feet four inches.

A tremendous cheer went up, and the crowd

surged forward. After two miserable years of battles and bloodshed with no end in sight, the people looked to their president for assurance that the nation would survive. He was their father figure.

A hastily assembled group of musicians struck up a ragged version of "Hail to the Chief." Lincoln waved some more and bowed to the crowd before him.

He was dressed simply, with a white shirt, black bow tie, and a plain black overcoat with three buttons on each side. His beard was neatly trimmed. He had no mustache.

The man next to Luke kept muttering angry things about the president. He appeared to be seething with hatred. To the rest of the crowd, Lincoln was a rock star. Men had hoisted their small children up on their shoulders so they could see the great Abraham Lincoln.

"God save our president!" somebody shouted.

Luke couldn't stop glancing over at the man next to him.

"Dude, I know I've seen that guy before," he whispered to David. "He's giving me the creeps."

"He probably just looks like somebody else," David replied.

The people on the street were happy to get a wave

from the president, but they wanted more.

"Speech! Speech!" a few began to chant.

Lincoln held up his hands. Little by little, the crowd began to settle down. The band stopped playing. A hush fell over the square.

"I appear before you, fellow citizens, merely to thank you for this compliment," the president said. His voice took everyone by surprise. They had expected it to be deep and somber, but it was unexpectedly high-pitched.

"Thank you for *nothing*," muttered the man next to Luke.

"The inference is a very fair one that you would hear me for a little while, at least, were I to commence to make a speech," said President Lincoln. "I do not appear before you for the purpose of doing so, and for several substantial reasons. The most substantial of these is that I have no speech to make."

The crowd laughed good-naturedly.

"It is somewhat important in my position that one should not say any foolish things if he can help it," he continued.

"If you can help it!" somebody shouted from the crowd, causing more laughter.

"It very often happens that the only way to help

it is to say nothing at all," said the president, which brought on more laughter.

The man next to Luke had closed his eyes, as if he was saying a silent prayer.

"Believing that is my present condition this evening," Lincoln continued, "I must beg of you to excuse me from addressing you further."

Lincoln bowed again and waved to the crowd some more. His little speech was over. The crowd burst into applause and celebration.

The man next to Luke was fiddling with something in his right pocket. That's when Luke figured out why his face seemed so familiar.

"It's John Wilkes Booth!" Luke said suddenly.

Luke was absolutely right. The angry man next to him was John Wilkes Booth, the well-known Shakespearean stage actor who would go on to assassinate President Lincoln two years later. Luke had seen a picture of him in his social studies textbook at school.

As Lincoln was turning to go back inside the Wills house, Booth pulled his right hand out of his pocket. There was a gun in it, and this one was *real*.

"That's *enough*," Booth muttered. "Now, by God, I'll put him through. This is the last speech *he'll* ever make."

I know what you're thinking, reader. You or I or *any* normal person under these circumstances would back away and separate ourselves from the dangerous situation. But sometimes, instinct takes over and the mind moves in the other direction.

"Get him, David!" Luke shouted, chopping down on Booth's arm to knock the gun loose. As he was doing that, David had come at Booth from the opposite side and punched him in the jaw. The two of them tried to wrestle Booth to the ground, but he was slippery and broke free from their grasp.

"Stop him!" David shouted.

But it was too late. Booth had escaped and was on the run, sneaking away around the corner, down an alley, and into the night.

CHAPTER 16

A BETTER IDEA

WITH ALL THE NOISE AND EXCITEMENT IN THE square, nobody else noticed there had been an attempt on the president's life. Everything happened so fast.

After finishing his short speech, President Lincoln waved to the crowd once more and ducked back inside the Wills house. The people roared with approval, then slowly began to disperse.

David and Luke continued to stand there, stunned.

"That's the second person we beat up today," David marveled, still staring at the front steps where Lincoln had been standing moments earlier.

"I can't believe we just saved the president's life,"

Luke replied. "We're heroes, dude. Unsung heroes. Nobody will know what we just did."

"You guys were awesome," Isabel told them.

"Don't be so impressed with yourselves," Julia told them. "Booth would have missed anyway."

"How do *you* know?" David asked.

"Because if he had killed the president, every history book would say he assassinated Lincoln at Gettysburg in 1863. But we all know it happened at Ford's Theatre in Washington in 1865."

"She's right," Luke admitted. "It didn't matter what we did to him. He would have missed."

"He's going to try it again in two years," David said. "And he's going to succeed. Nothing we can do about that."

"Maybe we can have Miss Z send us back in two years and stop the *real* assassination," Isabel suggested.

"I'm not sure I want to go through this again," Luke said. "I thought we were just going to come to Gettysburg, take the picture, and go home. I wasn't expecting all this fighting and stuff."

"Or . . ." David whispered, looking around, ". . . we could find Booth and kill him *now*. Then he won't have the chance to do *anything* in two years."

"Are you crazy?" Luke asked. "I'm not gonna kill anybody, not even John Wilkes Booth. Besides, we're under strict orders not to do *anything* that could change history, remember?"

The Flashback Four headed off down Baltimore Street looking for food and lodging for the night. They hadn't gone more than a few steps when Julia spotted a couple of boys walking toward them—the same boys they had encountered earlier. This time they were carrying some packages. Julia elbowed Isabel, and the two of them started to giggle. Luke groaned.

"So we meet again, ladies!" the taller of the boys said cheerfully as he removed his hat and bowed deeply. He acted as though Luke and David weren't there.

"Well, howdy to *you*," Julia replied with a curtsy. "What brings you nice fellas out on this lovely evenin'?"

"We're delivering a heap of bread to the Gettysburg Hotel," the shorter one said. "Would you ladies like to accompany us?"

"Oh, ah don't know," Isabel said, blushing. "We're not supposed to cavort with strangers."

"We have other plans," Luke told the boys curtly.

"But we would sure like some bread."

The bread smelled *so* good. It smelled like it had just come out of the oven, because it *had* just come out of the oven. It had been a long time since any of the Flashback Four had smelled freshly baked *anything*. They were used to getting baked goods from the supermarket—wrapped, sealed in plastic, and shot full of preservatives.

"Oh, gee, we don't have any money," Isabel said, taking a deep sniff of the bread.

"I reckon we could spare one loaf for the pretty ladies," the taller boy said. "Just don't tell anybody, okay?"

"Our lips are sealed," Julia replied, giggling.

"Huh?" the two boys said, puzzled.

Julia had no idea that the expression "our lips are sealed" would not be coined for nearly fifty years.

"We'll keep it to ourselves," Isabel told them. "We are much obliged for your generosity."

The boys handed over a loaf of bread, and Isabel accepted it gratefully.

"Maybe we'll see you ladies at the parade tomorrow?" the shorter boy asked.

"Well, I reckon that maybe you *will*!" Julia said, giggling some more as she batted her eyelashes.

As soon as the boys were gone, Isabel broke the loaf into four pieces and passed them around. The Flashback Four wolfed them down as if they had never tasted bread before. That would satisfy their hunger, at least for a while.

The next order of business was to find a place to stay for the night. Coincidentally, the TTT buzzed in Isabel's pocket. She showed the others the message from Miss Z.

FIND A PLACE TO SLEEP?

"Tell her we're staying at the Hilton," David suggested.

NOT YET, Isabel typed.

Bzzz. A few seconds later, the reply came back—
TRY A CHURCH.

It was actually a good idea. During the Battle of Gettysburg, most of the churches in town had been converted into hospitals to handle all the wounded soldiers. It would make sense for the churches to be used now to house out-of-town visitors.

The Flashback Four continued walking down Baltimore Street. In four blocks, at the corner of High Street, they came to Gettysburg Presbyterian Church. It had originally been built as a log cabin back in 1740, three miles away. The congregation moved in 1842. It's still at the corner of Baltimore and High Streets today.

The kids climbed the steps. Luke was elected to do the talking. When he pulled open the front door, a minister blocked his entrance.

"Excuse me, we're mighty tuckered out and we're looking for a place to—"

"I'm terribly sorry," the minister told Luke. "We have over a hundred people sleeping here already. We don't have room for anyone else."

"Just four more?" asked Isabel. "We'll sleep on the pews if we have to."

"That's where everyone else is sleeping," the priest told her. "I'm sorry, Miss. You'll have to mosey along."

Discouraged, the group retreated back down the steps. There were other people wandering around, clearly looking for somewhere to spend the night.

"I bet every church in town is filled," Julia said.

"Let's get off the main drag," Isabel suggested. "Everybody's looking for a place to stay here."

They turned the corner on High Street. Soon the storefronts and official buildings were replaced by houses and fields. The gas lamps were replaced by moonlight. The night was warm and clear.

"These people need to invent the lightbulb, quick," David said. "I can't see *anything* out here."

"I'm afraid I'm gonna step in more horse poop," said Julia.

They walked past a few houses, but nobody had the courage to knock on a door and ask a total stranger if they could sleep there.

"Look," Isabel suddenly said as they approached a large building. "A barn!"

"I'm not sleeping in a *barn*!" Julia complained.

"Why not?" David asked.

"Animals sleep in barns," Julia said.

"Well if it's good enough for animals, it's good enough for me," Luke said. "I'm *tired*."

"No you're not," David told him. "You're tuckered out."

Julia stood on the dirt road as the others went to pull open the heavy barn door.

"You can find someplace else to sleep," Luke told her. "But we're staying here."

Julia ran to catch up.

It was almost pitch-dark inside the barn, but Isabel was able to find an empty horse stall with hay on the floor that would provide some small degree of comfort.

"It smells in here," Julia complained. "I bet there are rats, too."

"I don't care," Luke said, rolling his jacket up to make

a little pillow for himself. "I'm snug as a bug in a rug."

David picked another corner of the stall and lay down there. That left Julia and Isabel standing awkwardly, with one problem in common—it was impossible to lie down in those gigantic dresses.

"We won't look," David assured them. "Can't see anything anyway."

"There's nothing to look at," Isabel said as she peeled off the dress. "I have like ten layers of clothes on underneath this thing."

Julia unhooked her dress too, and as she did something fell out of it and bonked David on the head.

"Oww!" he shouted. "What was *that*?"

"Oops," Julia said.

It only took David a few seconds to figure out what had fallen out of Julia's dress. It was a gun. In fact, it was John Wilkes Booth's gun.

"What are you doing with *this*?" David demanded, sitting up and rubbing the side of his face.

"I didn't steal it!" Julia explained. "It was just lying on the ground. So I picked it up. Finders keepers."

"It was lying on the ground because we knocked it out of Booth's hand!" Luke yelled.

"Are you crazy?" Isabel shouted at Julia. "That thing is loaded. You could have killed David!"

"But look, you guys," Julia said. "Think about it. This gun belonged to John Wilkes Booth. The *real* John Wilkes Booth! Do you have any idea how much it might be worth? We could sell it on eBay and make *thousands*. Maybe more. I'll split the money with you."

"No!" David said, putting the gun in his corner of the stall. "Miss Z told us *no* souvenirs. This thing is dangerous. What if it had gone off when it hit me?"

"Okay, okay, I'm sorry!" Julia said, in a way that told the others that she wasn't really sorry at all.

"What is wrong with you?" Isabel asked, as she curled up on the floor. "Is money *that* important?"

"Sometimes I can't control myself," Julia admitted.

"Let's talk about it tomorrow," Isabel said. "I'm going to sleep."

"G'night, you guys," muttered David.

Each member of the Flashback Four settled into a

corner of the stall. They were exhausted and the barn was perfectly quiet. But it was hard to sleep because it had been such an exciting day. There was a lot to think about.

"Hey, Luke," Julia whispered after five minutes of tossing and turning.

"What?"

"Remember when I was trying to steal the Gettysburg Address and take it home to make money?"

"Yeah."

"You said you had a better idea."

"Yeah, I did."

"What was it?"

"Yeah, what *was* that better idea?" David asked.

Luke sat up.

"I've been thinking about it a lot," he said, lowering his voice to a whisper. "Do any of you guys know when Thomas Edison invented the phonograph?"

"Nope," David said. "Who cares?"

"It was 1877," Luke told him. "That's fourteen years from now."

"So?" asked Isabel. "What does that have to do with anything?"

"Well," Luke explained, "Edison recorded sound for the first time ever in 1877. So any sound that was made before that year was lost forever."

"Go on," David said, sitting up against the wall.

"So I was thinking," Luke said, becoming more excited as he continued, "Lincoln was killed in 1865. Nobody in our time knows what Lincoln's voice sounded like, because there was no way to record sound in his lifetime."

"And the camera Miss Z gave us can shoot video, right?" Isabel said.

"And *audio*," replied Luke. "We can *film* the Gettysburg Address tomorrow and bring home the only audio recording of Abraham Lincoln's voice! How much money do you think *that* might be worth?"

"You're right!" said Julia.

"And the beauty of it is, we don't have to bring anything home except the camera," Luke said, "which we're bringing home with us anyway. We don't have to change history. We don't have to steal anything. I just have to push the button."

"You are a *genius*!" David said.

"Don't mention it."

Nobody did. One by one, the Flashback Four dropped off to sleep, dreaming of making history, and making millions.

LOOK WHAT I FOUND

LUKE, DAVID, ISABEL, AND JULIA WERE AWAKENED in the morning by the sound of a rooster crowing.

Cock-a-doodle-dooooo . . .

"Are you kidding me?" Julia moaned, covering her ears. "They really *do* that? I thought it was just something roosters did in cartoons."

"No, they actually do it," Luke said. "My grandfather grew up on a farm."

"I need more sleep," Julia groaned.

"I need something to eat," Isabel said.

"I need a shower," said David, "and I want to brush my teeth."

It was Thursday, November 19, 1863, and the sunlight streaming into the barn promised it was going to be a good day. It was the *right* day, at least. This was the day that Abraham Lincoln would deliver the Gettysburg Address, less than a mile away.

A moment after the rooster crowed, the kids were jolted by another sound—a bugle call, followed by a series of thundering explosions echoing in the distance.

"What is *that*?" asked Isabel. "Is there another battle going on?"

Julia and Isabel hurriedly put their dresses on and joined the boys, who had already hustled outside to find out what was going on. They couldn't see it, but on Cemetery Ridge, a section of the Gettysburg battlefield, a sixteen-round artillery salute was being fired in honor of President Lincoln. He and Secretary of State Seward were getting an early-morning tour of the battlefield, with all the military ceremony deserving of a president. After his tour was over, Lincoln would be taken back to the Wills house, and the parade to the cemetery was scheduled to begin at ten o'clock.

The air was crisp, but not cold. In the light of day, the kids could see that the barn they had slept in was at the corner of a large farm. Fields of pumpkins, turnips, and other crops could be seen stretching into the distance.

There was a shovel leaning against the barn. Luke used it to dig a small hole in the ground. David threw in the gun they had knocked out of John Wilkes Booth's hand the night before and covered it with dirt.

"This stays *here*," Luke said to Julia sternly. "Understand?"

"Yeah," she mumbled.

Luke's idea made more sense anyway, and Julia knew it. Instead of trying to sell Booth's gun to make money, they could record the Gettysburg Address with Miss Z's camera. The video and audio would be worth millions, and the modern world would get the chance to hear the sound of Abraham Lincoln's voice for the first time. They wouldn't be taking back any souvenirs—other than some electrons on a computer chip. There was nothing illegal about it. They wouldn't be changing history in any way. They would just be observing and recording it. And they would still be able to get a photo of Lincoln delivering his speech for Miss Z. It seemed like a perfect plan.

Bzzz. Isabel felt the buzz of the TTT in her pocket.

GOOD MORNING, the message read. THIS IS YOUR WAKEUP CALL.

WE ALREADY GOT A WAKEUP CALL, Isabel typed back.

"Don't tell her about the new plan," Julia said.

Bzzz.

PARADE TO CEMETERY BEGINS AT 10, Miss Z texted. LINCOLN SPEECH AT 2.

"How are we supposed to know what time it is?" Julia asked. "She has our cell phones."

"It's around seven o'clock in the morning," Luke said, looking at the horizon in the distance.

"How do *you* know?"

Indeed, how did Luke know what time it was? It had never occurred to the others that you could get a sense of what time it was by the elevation of the sun in the sky. For centuries, that's what people did to tell time. We're so used to watches, clocks, and cell phones that we are sometimes hopeless without them.

"I'm starved," David said.

"It's a *farm*," Luke told him. "There's food all over the place."

"Is this legal?" Isabel asked as they wandered into the field. "Isn't it stealing if we take something from here without asking?"

"There's nobody around," David said. "Besides, we won't eat much."

There were tall corn stalks all around, but the ears

had been picked clean during the summer, when corn was in season. Deeper in the field, they came upon a smaller garden.

"Berries!" Luke said, just about diving into them.

There were rows of huckleberries, black crow-berries, cape gooseberries, and others. Luke started picking them off the vines and stuffing them in his mouth.

"How do you know they're not poisonous?" Julia asked.

"Why would a farmer grow poisonous berries?" Luke asked, the juice running down his chin.

"To keep people like us from eating them?" David guessed.

But after seeing Luke enjoying the feast and not toppling over, David got down on his knees and began picking berries himself. Isabel did the same.

"Hey, these are *good*!" she said, filling her mouth.

Julia stood back a few feet, watching them.

"That stuff grows in *dirt*," she said, wrinkling up her nose. "That's where the word *dirty* comes from. I've never eaten anything that didn't come in a package."

"So don't eat it," David told her. "More for us."

In the end, even Julia consented to trying the ber-ries, and she enjoyed them as much as the others did.

When they'd had their fill, the Flashback Four walked deeper into the field to see what else might be on the menu. What they found strewn about, however, were mainly fragments of war-ragged knapsacks, canteens, shoes, holsters, clothing, and other belongings that had been left behind by soldiers who had fought there four months earlier.

After a few minutes, they detected a smell, faint at first, and then powerful and pungent as they got closer. On the ground next to a large maple tree, they discovered the rotting corpse of a horse. Everybody gasped at the sight of it.

"Ugh," Luke said, covering his nose and mouth. "That guy didn't make it."

"The poor thing," Isabel said.

"I think I may throw up," said Julia.

I know what you're thinking, reader. What was a dead horse doing there? Good question. In addition to all the men who were wounded or killed at Gettysburg, five thousand horses and mules were casualties of the battle. Burying them was out of the question. Most of the large animals had to be doused with oil and incinerated where they fell. But the horses that had the misfortune to die right next to a house or a tree couldn't be set on fire. There was nothing to do but let them rot on the ground.

"I say we get out of here," David suggested.

The farm was quite large, and it was hard for the kids to retrace their steps back to the barn and the main road where they had started. They set off in the wrong direction at first, walking single file through a row of tomato plants. David led the way, so it was David who stubbed his toe on a large gray object that was half-buried in the dirt. It was shaped like a two-liter soda bottle. David bent down to pick it up.

"Hey, check out this old bottle," he told the others. "This thing is *heavy*!"

"Just drop it," Luke advised.

"DON'T DROP IT!"

The voice was rough, loud, and urgent. It came from behind them. David was so startled that he nearly dropped the thing he had just been warned not to drop.

All four kids turned around. There was a heavy man with a beard standing behind them, and he was holding a shotgun.

"Oh no, not *again*!" David groaned.

"We're sorry, sir," Isabel said quickly. "We ate some

of your berries. We were hungry and we didn't have any money."

"DON'T DROP THAT!" the man repeated, just a little more calmly.

He rested his shotgun on the ground and approached David cautiously.

"That ain't no bottle, son," he said. "It's a shell. And I reckon it just might be a live one."

"You mean, the kind of shell that *explodes*?" Julia asked.

"Well, it ain't exploded *yet*," the man replied. "But it could blow anytime."

David looked terrified.

In case you don't know, a shell is basically an explosive charge packed with gunpowder and wrapped by an iron casing. Some were designed to detonate in midair. Others had a percussion fuse, so they would detonate on impact. Either way, the shell would burst into a dozen or so iron fragments that were designed to rip through human flesh.

Thousands of shells were fired in the Battle of Gettysburg. Some of them landed in fields without exploding, to be discovered days, months, or even years later.

"Maybe it's a dud," David said hopefully, holding the shell at arm's length.

"You willin' to bet your life on that?" the man asked.

"Okay, okay!" David said. "So what should I do with it?"

"Follow me," the man said. "And don't trip over nothin' and fall down with that thing in your hands, you hear? That could be the end of you."

As they walked, the man said his name was Big Jim and that he owned the farm. He didn't mind the kids eating a few of his berries, but he said he sure didn't want them blowing themselves up on his land. This was the third unexploded shell he'd found on his property since the battle ended.

These days, of course, bomb squads have sophisticated techniques they use to defuse bombs. But Big Jim had a simpler idea. He led the Flashback Four across the field and down the road until they reached a wooden fence. On the other side of the fence was a steep drop into a narrow ditch.

"Can you throw good?" Big Jim asked David. "You got a good arm on you?"

"Sure, I can sink a shot from half-court, nothing but net," David replied, not realizing that basketball was twenty-eight years away from being invented.

"Ah don't know what in tarnation that means," Big Jim replied. "But I'm gonna need you to chuck that shell as far as you can into that gully over yonder. Think you can manage that?"

"I'll try."

"I'd do it myself, but I got me a bum arm," Big Jim said.

"Is it going to blow up?" Isabel asked.

"That's what we're gonna find out," Big Jim replied. "Let 'er rip, son."

All eyes turned to David. He took a deep breath. The others backed up to give him room.

"Okay, here goes nothing," he said.

David spun around a few times like an Olympic discus thrower. Then he let the shell fly with a grunt, heaving it high in the air.

"Now duck!" Big Jim shouted.

Boom!

Nobody saw the explosion. But they heard it, and saw the dirt flying. It was a long time until the sound stopped echoing across the fields.

CHAPTER 18

A NEW BIRTH OF FREEDOM

"WELL, YOU DON'T SEE *THAT* EVERY DAY," ISABEL said after everybody had picked themselves up, dusted themselves off, and checked to see if any body parts were missing.

"Everybody all right?" asked Big Jim.

"I'm fit as a fiddle!" David replied.

It was past eight o'clock in the morning and the kids were anxious to see the parade to the cemetery. They were also anxious to shoot the video of Lincoln and go home.

But when Big Jim *insisted* that they come into his house, meet his wife, and have breakfast, it was hard to refuse. Mrs. Big Jim (they never did catch her name) was lovely, and seemed to effortlessly put together a spread of eggs, bacon, biscuits, potatoes, and some kind of stuff that none of the kids could identify but ate anyway just to be polite. It was all delicious and really hit the spot.

Big Jim and his wife didn't have any children of their own, so they took a special delight when kids came around to visit. As they chatted over breakfast, the Flashback Four were extra careful not to mention the internet, microwave popcorn, Cartoon Network, Froot Loops, or any other references that might be incomprehensible to people in the nineteenth century.

"Well, we've got to go, uh, boil our shirts," David told Big Jim and his wife. "But we're much obliged for this fine breakfast."

By the time they got back to Baltimore Street, it was jam-packed with people, most of them heading north toward the square. Men, women, and children were decked out in their finest attire. Military bands were marching up the street in formation, looking sharp. American flags were everywhere, hanging outside each building and being waved around by people of all ages.

The Flashback Four fell in step with the crowd. The

atmosphere felt different than it had the day before. It wasn't a party anymore. People looked more somber, and for good reason. On this day, the president of the United States had come to honor the soldiers who had died at Gettysburg four months earlier.

Luke turned on the camera and checked the controls. Everything seemed to be working. Just to be on the safe side, he fired off a few practice shots. Then he turned the camera off to avoid draining the battery.

It seemed like everybody in town had gathered at the square for the parade to the cemetery. It was a huge crowd.

"I bet John Wilkes Booth is out here somewhere," David said, looking around nervously.

"Yeah, but we took away his gun," Luke reminded him, "and I don't think he's gonna find it."

"What if he has *another* gun?" asked Julia.

"Look, we don't have to worry about Booth," Luke reminded them. "If he tries anything today, we *know* he's going to fail. If he succeeded, it would be in the history books, right?"

"Yeah," David said, "but what if his other gun is better than the one we took away from him? Then we changed history and he shoots Lincoln with his other gun."

"I think my head is going to explode," Luke replied. "We can't worry about that stuff."

At precisely ten o'clock, the front door of the Wills house opened and President Lincoln appeared in the doorway. Polite applause washed across the square as people stopped, pointed, and whispered to their neighbors. There were no raucous cheers or drunken hooting. Not today.

Lincoln was dressed, as usual, in a plain black suit, bow tie, and stovepipe hat. For this special occasion, he also held a pair of white gloves in his hand. He had a serious look on his face as he reached out to shake hands with a few people who had the courage to approach him. A little boy was rewarded with a pat on the head.

As he ambled down the steps, the president moved awkwardly, almost like a man on stilts. He walked slowly between two lines of soldiers until he got to a reddish-brown horse, which had been specially selected to carry him to the cemetery. The horse was quite short, and when Lincoln mounted it, his feet nearly touched the ground. It was comical looking, and on a different day people might have laughed at the sight of such a tall man on a short horse.

"I wonder where Tad is," Isabel whispered.

"Oh, I'm sure that little troublemaker is around here somewhere," replied Julia.

It took a long time to organize all the various marchers into a parade line. In front of the president, a five-man color guard waving huge American flags led the way to Baltimore Street. The Marine Band followed them, playing a crisp march. After that came a squadron of cavalry, two batteries of artillery, and a regiment of infantry soldiers. They were followed by marshals on horseback wearing black suits decorated with white sashes. Behind them was the Second United States Artillery Band, blasting away with trumpets and drums.

The president's horse looked anxious to get going, prancing back and forth in place, much to the crowd's delight. When he finally got the signal, Lincoln snapped the reins and bowed his head to the left and right to acknowledge the applause from the citizens lining both sides of the street.

The parade moved slowly, because there were so many marchers. Following Lincoln was a large group of generals, congressmen, governors, clergymen, dignitaries, and prominent citizens like David Wills, who had graciously invited the president to stay at his home the night before. Behind that group was a line of local civic organizations and professors from Gettysburg College. Finally, bringing up the rear were dozens of soldiers who had been wounded in battle, many of them walking with crutches and canes.

The Flashback Four were following the crowd down Baltimore Street when Isabel felt the now familiar vibration of the TTT in her pocket. *Bzzz*.

ARE YOU AT THE CEMETERY? asked Miss Z.

ON OUR WAY, Isabel typed back.

"We'd better hurry up," she told the others. "We need to get to the front of these people if we're going to get a good position to shoot the video."

"That's right!" Luke said, slapping his forehead. "Let's move!"

He started jogging down the street, dodging left and right around marchers like a running back. David was right behind him, and the girls—with their giant dresses—struggled to keep up.

About midway through the parade line, two smiling boys jumped in front of Julia and Isabel. They were the same boys who had been flirting with them the night before.

"Well, hello again!" the taller one said cheerfully. "We hoped we would see you ladies here. I hope you enjoyed the bread."

"Isn't it a most spectacular day for a parade?" asked the shorter one. "If you two would care to join us, we're fixin' to—"

"Can't talk now," Julia shouted as she hustled past the boys. Then, feeling a little guilty about taking their bread, Julia added, "My cell is 617-555-0143. Text me!"

The two boys stared blankly at the girls as they disappeared into the crowd.

"You realize, of course," Isabel told Julia, "that the telephone hasn't been invented yet. And there won't be any cell phones or text messages for over a *hundred* years."

"That's *their* problem," Julia replied.

The four rushed toward the front of the parade as it continued down Baltimore Street. The road split after a few blocks, and the leaders of the parade turned at Emmitsburg Road to enter Soldiers' National Cemetery. Hundreds of people were already there, having come early to stake out positions close to the speaker's platform.

This cemetery, I want you to know, was different from most military cemeteries. Usually, the officers are buried in one section and the foot soldiers in a separate section. But in the Soldiers' National Cemetery, everyone was treated equally. The graves were grouped by state. So all the fallen soldiers from Massachusetts, for example, were buried in one area, and all the ones from New Jersey in another area. Of the eighteen states that were represented, the one with the most graves was New York. Almost a quarter of all the graves belonged to soldiers from that state.

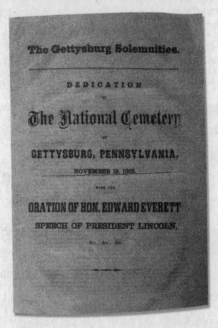

The Gettysburg Solemnities.

DEDICATION

OF

The National Cemetery

AT

GETTYSBURG, PENNSYLVANIA,

NOVEMBER 19, 1863.

WITH THE

ORATION OF HON. EDWARD EVERETT

SPEECH OF PRESIDENT LINCOLN,

&c., &c., &c.

As they entered the cemetery, the Flashback Four were careful not to step on any graves. It was important to show respect for the dead, which was what this day was all about. A group of soldiers held up a banner honoring their comrades who had died in the battle.

Two men ushered President Lincoln and his little horse toward the speaker's platform, where he dismounted, and then the horse was led away. The stage was made of wood, about three feet high and the size of a large room. Three rows of chairs had been set up on it, with ten chairs in each row. Gradually they were filled with dignitaries, including the governors of Pennsylvania, New Jersey, Indiana, Maine, Maryland, Ohio, and West Virginia. At the front of the stage was a small wooden table with a pitcher of water on it.

Luke noticed that there was no podium, and more importantly, no microphone. In 1863, public speakers had to project their voice if they wanted to be heard. That could be a problem for the video Luke was planning to shoot.

President Lincoln took his seat—a high-backed rocking chair—in the middle of the front row. Secretary of State Seward sat to his left. The seat on his other side was empty, for the time being.

At the side of the stage, a line of newspaper reporters were already waiting with pencils and paper in hand, ready to jot down every word spoken. Scattered around the crowd were several photographers, setting up their big, bulky cameras. Seeing them reminded

Luke of the importance of his mission. None of those photographers was going to capture Lincoln delivering the Gettysburg Address. So he would *have* to.

"You nervous?" David asked Luke.

"Yeah, a little. I don't want to mess this up."

David patted Luke on the shoulder.

A band played a somber dirge to set the mood. The crowd pushed forward as more people filled the cemetery grounds. There must have been fifteen or twenty thousand all together. The Flashback Four were all jammed together. It looked like it would be impossible to move.

The music came to an end. There was restless anticipation throughout the crowd. The people sensed that the ceremony was about to begin. Luke held the camera low but at the ready. He wanted to wait until the last possible moment to hold it up in the air.

A clergyman, the Reverend Thomas Stockton, walked to the front of the stage. The men in the crowd removed their hats without being told. Luke and David followed suit. A hush fell over the cemetery.

"Our Father, which art in heaven, hallowed be thy Name . . ."

At the end of the Lord's Prayer, Reverend Stockton praised the Union soldiers who had fought so bravely at Gettysburg.

"As the trees are not dead, though their foliage is gone," he said, "so our heroes are not dead, though their forms have fallen."

A choir sang a hymn that was unfamiliar to the Flashback Four, but the crowd knew it well and joined in. Some people were moved to tears.

The reverend went back to his seat at the back of the stage. Luke got ready to raise the camera, expecting President Lincoln to stand up and deliver the Gettysburg Address. But he didn't.

Instead, an elderly, white-haired man emerged from a small tent not far from the stage. He was escorted up the steps and over to the empty seat on Lincoln's right. When he sat down, everyone else on the stage rose from their seats as a sign of respect, including the president.

"Who's the old dude?" Luke whispered in David's ear.

"Beats me. He's sure making a grand entrance."

The old dude was Edward Everett, who was actually the featured speaker of the day. You probably thought the main attraction was Abraham Lincoln. Most people think that. But the president was only asked to give a few "appropriate remarks" at the dedication. It was Edward Everett who was to give the main speech. He's nearly forgotten now, but in his day Everett was one of the most famous orators in the world.

You're probably wondering, reader, why Everett made such a grand entrance. The truth is that he had bladder problems, and needed to use the bathroom frequently. A little toilet had been set up inside the tent so the great man would not have to interrupt the ceremonies to pee.

Luke relaxed a bit and put the camera down as Everett stood up and walked slowly to the center of the stage. The audience quieted down. Everett rested his speech on the small table in front of him, but he never looked at it. He began to speak from memory. . . .

"Standing beneath this serene sky, overlooking these broad fields . . ."

Edward Everett began his speech by talking about how the ancient Greeks had honored their soldiers who died in wars. It was difficult to hear his voice, especially for those unlucky enough to be at the back of the crowd. A few people near the stage began relaying the words—sentence by sentence—to people behind them, so the speech got passed through the crowd, like a game of telephone.

"This might be a problem," Luke whispered to Isabel. "I don't know if the camera is going to pick up Lincoln's voice from this distance."

"Let's try to get closer," she replied.

Holding hands to stay together, the Flashback Four elbowed their way past the people in front of them, causing a few dirty looks and stepped-on toes. Onstage, Edward Everett was going on and on about the Battle of Gettysburg, describing every thrust and parry, every strategic move by the Union and Confederate armies, with great emotion. It looked like he was settling in for the long haul.

Luke decided it would be a good idea to test the camera again. He turned it on and held it up, but not so high that it would attract attention from the rest of the crowd, who had never seen such a device.

It looked like the video and audio were coming through fine. Luke flashed a quick thumbs-up sign to the others. He was now in a good position for filming.

Everett went on talking at length about the Battle of Gettysburg. After an hour, he was showing no signs of reaching the end. Still, the audience hung on to his every word. People had longer attention spans in those days.

"Is this guy *ever* going to wrap it up?" Julia whispered.

"He might die of old age first," David cracked.

Bzzz. Isabel felt the TTT vibrating in her pocket.

DID YOU TAKE THE SHOT? Miss Z asked.

SOME OLD GUY IS TALKING, Isabel typed back.

Everett had finished his description of the battle and had moved on to discuss what was going to happen after the Civil War was over. He took fifteen minutes to basically predict that America would be stronger than ever.

As I'm sure you know, standing for a long period of time is hard on your legs and back. The crowd seemed to be getting restless, and as an experienced orator,

Everett could sense it. He had started talking at noon, and had been at it for nearly two hours. It was warmer outside now. People were removing their coats. Some had already left the grounds and gone home. Everett started to wind down his speech.

Behind him, President Lincoln took a pair of glasses from his pocket and put them on. Then he pulled out three sheets of paper—the same sheets Julia had found in his room the day before.

"This is it," David whispered to Luke. "Be ready."

Lincoln appeared to be nervous as he looked over what he had written. The address he was about to deliver was not just some *howdy-do-folks, nice-to-be-here* kind of speech. It was serious stuff. Thousands of Americans had already died in this awful war, and thousands more would die before it was over. People had lost their sons, their brothers, and their fathers. The president wanted to explain to the citizens why such a terrible price needed to be paid to fight against their own countrymen. He returned the sheets of paper to his pocket.

You may be wondering, reader, if Lincoln mentioned slavery in his Gettysburg Address. He didn't. Not once. But that's what the speech was about. The outcome of the war would determine whether or not a nation that was dedicated to the idea that all men are created equal could survive.

Without saying it out loud, Lincoln was about to tell the crowd—and the nation—that America could have slavery or liberty, but not both. Having liberty doesn't mean you have the liberty to enslave other people. Having freedom doesn't mean you have the freedom to take away somebody else's freedom.

Essentially, Lincoln would be proposing a *new* nation. And he would be telling Americans—mostly *white* Americans—that this new nation was worth fighting for.

Finally, after two solid hours of nonstop talking, Edward Everett wrapped things up.

> *"As we bid farewell to the dust of these martyr-heroes, that wheresoever throughout the civilized world the accounts of this great warfare are read, and down to the latest period of recorded time, in the glorious annals of our common country there will be no brighter page than that which relates the Battles of Gettysburg."*

The crowd rewarded the old man with a thunderous ovation. Or maybe they were just happy that he was finished talking. Lincoln shook Everett's hand and thanked him. Everett was helped off stage, where he trudged over to his little tent to use the bathroom. He had been holding it in for a long time.

"Okay, you gotta be quick," David whispered to Luke. "Once Lincoln starts talking, the whole thing will be over in two minutes."

"I know, dude. I know," Luke said, gripping the camera tightly.

It looked like the president was about to stand up, but instead, the Baltimore Glee Club sang another hymn. Then, some guy with a top hat announced, "Ladies and gentlemen, the president of the United States of America."

Lincoln removed his hat, put it on the floor under his seat, and stood up. The crowd applauded enthusiastically as he walked to the front of the stage. The battlefield where those soldiers had fought so bravely was spread out in front of him. Behind him was their final resting place. He stood silent for a moment, his hands clasped together and his head bowed.

Luke turned on the camera.

Or, he *tried* to turn on the camera, anyway. He was fumbling with the buttons.

"Something's wrong!" he muttered under his breath.

"What do you mean something's wrong?" Julia asked, alarmed.

"It won't turn on!" Luke said.

"Did you push the right button?" David asked.

"Of *course* I pushed the right button!" Luke said as he frantically fiddled with the camera. "I'm not stupid!"

Lincoln waited for the applause to die down. Then he took the three sheets of paper out of his pocket and unfolded them. He didn't put his speech on the table, the way Everett had. He held it in his hand.

A hush fell over the crowd. Lincoln had a solemn look on his face. Luke was still fumbling with the camera.

"Four score and seven years ago . . ."

"You missed the beginning!" Julia said to Luke, poking him.

"our fathers brought forth on this continent a new nation, conceived in liberty, and dedicated to the proposition that all men are created equal . . ."

Lincoln was speaking very slowly and clearly, in a Kentucky accent. Meanwhile, Luke and the others were freaking out.

"Why do they make these things so hard to use?" Luke muttered.

"I thought you knew how to use the thing!" Julia said.

"I *did*."

Cheers and applause washed over the audience when Lincoln spoke the words "all men are created equal." He had to stop and wait until the hubbub trailed off before he could continue.

"Now we are engaged in a great civil war, testing whether that nation, or any nation so conceived and so dedicated, can long endure . . ."

His speech was mostly memorized, but the president glanced down at his papers several times. He spoke without making gestures.

Sweat was dripping down Luke's forehead as he tried to get the camera to work.

"I should have brought my cell phone," Julia said. "We would have the video right now."

"Maybe the battery's dead," Isabel guessed.

"How can it be dead?" Luke asked. "I didn't use it at all, hardly."

"Batteries drain even when you don't use them," said David.

Lincoln glanced up briefly to scan the crowd before continuing.

"We are met on a great battlefield of that war. We have come to dedicate a portion of that field, as a final resting place for those who here gave their lives that that nation might live. It is altogether fitting and proper that we should do this . . ."

"You should have charged up the battery," Julia told Luke.

"Where was he gonna charge it?" David replied. "You see any electrical outlets around here?"

"Maybe I had the camera on the whole time Everett was talking," Luke grumbled.

"Why would you do that?" asked Isabel.

"I didn't do it on purpose! Stop yelling at me! You're not helping!"

A lady next to the Flashback Four put a finger to her lips and shot them a disapproving look.

"Shhhhh!" she said.

"But, in a larger sense, we can not dedicate—we can not consecrate—we can not hallow—this ground. The brave men, living and dead, who struggled here, have consecrated it, far above our poor power to add or detract . . ."

The crowd broke into applause again, causing Lincoln to stop.

"Hurry up!" Julia whispered to Luke. "Figure it out!"

"Shut up!"

"*You* shut up!"

"Forget the video!" David whispered. "It's too late now. Put it on still pictures and try to turn it on. We gotta get the shot for Miss Z, at least."

"The world will little note, nor long remember what we say here, but it can never forget what they did here . . ."

Lincoln swept his hand in a wide circle across the field of graves. For a moment, he was choked up. The crowd applauded again. People nodded their heads in agreement.

Time was running out. Luke's hands had become slippery as he fumbled with the camera.

"Miss Z is gonna freak out!" Isabel whispered.

"It is for us the living, rather, to be dedicated here to the unfinished work which they who fought here have thus far so nobly advanced . . ."

More applause.

"I give up," Luke said. "It's dead. I can't make it work."

"Don't give up!" Isabel said. "You can do this!"

"It is rather for us to be here dedicated to the great task remaining before us—that from these honored dead we take increased devotion to that cause for which they gave the last full measure of devotion . . ."

There were only a few seconds left in the speech.

"that we here highly resolve that these dead shall not have died in vain . . ."

Applause.

Luke gnashed his teeth. All the preparation and

everything they had been through since they arrived at Gettysburg had been for nothing. And they wouldn't be able to come back to try again because the Board could only send them to a specific time period once.

"that this nation, under God, shall have a new birth of freedom . . ."

Suddenly, for reasons unexplained, the little screen on the camera lit up.

"It's working!" Luke said.

"Quick! Take a still shot!" David said. "He's almost done!"

Luke held the camera up in the air over his head and pointed it in the direction of Abraham Lincoln.

"and that government of the people, by the people, for the people, shall not perish from the . . ."

As the president spoke the final word of the Gettysburg Address, Luke pushed the button.

"That young man has a weapon!" somebody shouted.

"He's trying to shoot the president!"

"Grab him!"

CHAPTER 19

A HEAP OF
TROUBLE

THREE BURLY BODYGUARDS CAME RUNNING OVER and pounced on Luke before he could get off another shot.

"Stop! Wait! Oww, you're hurting me!" he hollered as they wrestled him to the ground.

When David, Isabel, and Julia tried to pull the bodyguards off Luke, they were swatted away like mosquitoes.

Meanwhile, President Lincoln had finished delivering the Gettysburg Address to a tremendous ovation, which drowned out the commotion going on just twenty feet in front of him. He was escorted from the stage, shaking hands with many of the dignitaries in the front row.

"Get the gun!" one of the bodyguards shouted, as another one punched Luke in the face. The boy was on the ground in the fetal position now, protecting his head. His face was already swelling up.

"Hey, leave him alone!" shouted David.

"There's been a misunderstanding!" yelled Isabel.

"It's not a gun!" Julia shouted. "It's a camera!"

Luke had stopped putting up any resistance, and the Nikon was next to him on the grass. One of the bodyguards picked it up and examined it, a puzzled expression on his face.

"Don't look like no gun to me," he said.

"I don't care *what* it looks like," said one of the other bodyguards, who grabbed the Nikon, threw it on the ground, and stomped on it with his boot.

"No!" all four kids shouted, but it was too late. The Nikon was busted into little pieces.

"Ain't gonna hurt nobody *now*," said the bodyguard who had destroyed the camera.

The Flashback Four slumped against one another, crushed. They had been through so much already— arriving on the wrong day, stepping in horse manure, getting caught trying to steal the Gettysburg Address, fighting the president's son, sleeping in a barn, almost getting blown up by a live shell, and now *this*. The camera was broken, they'd failed at the one task they had been assigned to complete, and Miss Z was not going to get the photo she wanted so badly. To make matters worse, the kids were now being arrested, with their hands cuffed behind their backs.

"I didn't do anything!" Julia shouted as she was led away.

"You were part of the conspiracy, young lady," one of the bodyguards told her. "That's as bad as pulling the trigger."

"There *was* no trigger!" shouted Isabel. "It wasn't even a gun!"

"You're making a big mistake!" shouted Luke as he was pushed from behind. "We're innocent!"

"Quit yer bellyachin', sonny! Tell it to the judge!"

While the others protested, David kept his mouth shut. As the only African American in the group, he was afraid that he would be treated even more harshly than the others if he put up any resistance.

Two blocks from the cemetery was the small county jail. The Flashback Four were led down the street and shoved roughly into a cell. The door slammed shut behind them with a loud *clang*. A large padlock clicked shut. Then the bodyguards left, leaving the kids by themselves.

It was dark and dingy, and it smelled musty in the jail cell. There was a filthy mattress on the floor, and nobody dared touch it. Luke slumped against the wall. He had a black eye, his face was bruised, and he was on the verge of tears. David came over to comfort him.

"It's gonna be okay," he said, resting a hand on Luke's shoulder. "We'll get out of this."

"This place is *gross*," Julia commented.

I know what you're thinking, reader. Are they even *allowed* to put kids in jail? Isn't that against the law? Wasn't it against the law in 1863? Whatever the case, the law didn't matter. They were locked in, and they weren't going anywhere.

"What are we gonna do *now*?" David whispered. "We're supposed to be at the square at three o'clock so Miss Z can zap us home, right?"

"Home?" Luke replied. "That's the *least* of our problems, dude! They may *hang* us. That's what they did to the people who helped John Wilkes Booth when he shot Lincoln. They hung 'em, in public."

"They might use a firing squad," Julia said.

"For all we know," said Luke, "they're still using the guillotine."

Julia touched her neck and gulped hard at the thought of it.

"They're not going to execute us," Isabel said, trying her best to be optimistic. "They don't execute kids."

"You don't know that for sure," David said.

"What are we gonna do?" Julia groaned.

The question hung in the air for a few moments as everyone tried to think of a way out of the mess.

"I got it!" Luke finally said, snapping his fingers. "The TTT! Send Miss Z a text, Isabel! Tell her to zap us out of here, *now*!"

"But she said she was going to zap us back from the main square at three o'clock," Isabel replied.

"Tell her there's been a change in plans," Luke said. "Maybe she can do it from here. At least give it a try. Quick!"

Isabel took the TTT out of her pocket. She was about to type on it when a uniformed man showed up on the other side of the bars. He had a badge that said SHERIFF on it.

"Well, lookee here," he said, sneering. "What are you, Rebel spies? They sure get 'em young these days."

"We're not spies, sir," Isabel said politely. "We're just regular kids. We didn't mean any harm to the—"

"Quiet!" the sheriff barked. "You sure don't look like no assassins. But maybe that's why they picked you. So we wouldn't suspect you. Them Rebs ain't dumb."

"I want a lawyer," said Luke. "We have the right to a lawyer."

"Oh, keep your britches on," the sheriff told him. "You got the right to nothin'."

"Aren't we supposed to get one phone call?" asked Julia.

"Yeah," David said glumly. "You can call up Alexander Graham Bell and tell him to invent the telephone."

As if on cue, the TTT began to vibrate in Isabel's hand. *Bzzz.* She quickly hid it behind her back.

"What in tarnation is that sound?" asked the sheriff.

"Nothing," Isabel said.

Bzzz.

"There it goes again," the sheriff said, looking at the kids one at a time. "Somethin's buzzin'."

Bzzz.

"What's that you're holdin' behind your back, Miss?" he asked Isabel.

"Nothing," she repeated.

"Give it over," the sheriff said, putting his hand through the bars.

"Don't give it to him, Isabel!" Luke told her. "It's the only chance we've got to get out of here!"

The sheriff grabbed at Isabel's arm and yanked it, causing the TTT to fall on the floor. Luke tried to kick it away, but the sheriff bent down quickly and picked it up first.

"What's this thing?" he asked.

"It's nothing," Luke said. "Leave her out of this."

"Did I ask *you*?" the sheriff said. "How's about you sit down and shut your mouth, son? I'll get to you in a minute."

The sheriff examined the TTT, turning it over like a seashell he had picked up off the beach.

Bzzz.

He almost dropped it. Then these words appeared on the little screen . . .

SO DID YOU TAKE THE SHOT?

The sheriff had never seen words scroll across a screen before. For that matter, he had never seen a *screen* before. He held it up to show it to the kids.

"If that don't beat all!" he said. "How'd them letters get there like that?"

"You wouldn't believe me if I told you," Isabel replied.

"It's electrons," said David. "It's like magic."

Bzzz. The first text disappeared and was replaced by another message . . .

DID YOU SHOOT LINCOLN YET?

"Oh no," Luke groaned.

The sheriff's eyes opened wide.

"Y-you don't understand," Isabel stammered. "It doesn't mean shoot as in *shoot*. It means—"

"Oh, you kids are in a *heap* of trouble," the sheriff said. Then he took the TTT, dropped it on the floor, and picked up a chair so he could use one of the legs to crush the TTT.

"No!" all the kids yelled. But it was no use.

Only after bashing it a few times was the sheriff satisfied that the device could never be used or fixed. The TTT had been rendered useless.

"So, you were gonna shoot the president, eh?" he said. "I reckon I better go get the mayor for this one. You four sit here and think about what you did. I'll be back in a minute."

The sheriff turned and walked away, slamming the front door of the jailhouse behind him.

It wasn't long before the entire Flashback Four were in tears. First it was Julia, then David. That set Isabel off, and soon Luke was crying too.

"I *knew* we never should have signed on to this," Luke said. "Now we'll spend the rest of our lives here. And that might not be very long."

"I was always one of the *good* kids," Isabel said, wiping her eyes. "I study hard so I can get good grades and go to college someday. I never did *anything* wrong. Ask *anybody*. I don't even jaywalk."

"As soon as that guy in the suit gave me the invitation, I felt like something was wrong," David said. "I never should've taken it. I should've thrown it in the garbage right then and there."

"We're never gonna get out of here," Julia said. "They're gonna kill us."

"Let's think positively," Luke said, seeing that somebody needed to step up and take charge of the situation. "What are we going to do now? There *must* be a way out of this."

"Maybe we can escape," David suggested, looking around the cell. "I bet we could find a way to bust out of here."

They didn't get the chance to try, because at that moment the sheriff came back with another man. He certainly didn't look like a mayor. His hair and clothes were all messed up, and he staggered toward the cell, almost hitting his head against the bars. He smelled of alcohol.

"Get in there, Charlie," the sheriff said as he removed the padlock, opened the cell door, and shoved the man inside. "You can sleep it off in here."

The sheriff went away again, and the man he'd called Charlie fell heavily on the mattress in the corner. Then he looked up, seeing the four kids for the first time. He had a wild look in his eyes.

"Don't talk to him," David advised his friends. "He looks crazy."

"What're you in for?" Charlie asked the kids.

"We're not in for *anything*," Luke replied. "It's all a big mistake."

"Mistake, eh?" Charlie said. "I made plenty of them in my time. You wanna hear about the biggest mistake I made?"

None of the kids replied, but Charlie didn't care. He was going to tell them no matter what. He struggled to his feet.

"When the battle was over, there was eight thousand dead bodies layin' all over town," Charlie said quietly. "They needed folks to bury 'em, so I volunteered. Big mistake."

"Why?" Isabel asked.

Charlie turned to face her.

"It was July," he said. "Stinkin' hot. And them

bodies were *everywhere*. Blood everywhere. Arms and legs everywhere."

"What do you mean?" David asked. "Why were there arms and legs everywhere?"

"'Cause them doctors were cuttin' 'em off left and right trying to save the lives of those boys," Charlie said. "But most of the time they couldn't save 'em, and there were just stacks of arms and legs layin' around."

"Ugh, *gross*," Julia said.

"We dug shallow graves," Charlie continued slowly, "and did our darndest to bury all those boys. But a few days later, the rains come and uncovered the bodies. Rottin' flesh. Wounds covered in worms. Flies all over. Then the hogs started eatin' 'em."

"Oh my God," Julia said. "I'm going to be sick."

"So we had to go and bury 'em all over again," Charlie continued. "You ever smell a body decomposin'?

We soaked our handkerchiefs in peppermint oil and held 'em to our noses, but it didn't help."

Charlie staggered back to the mattress in the corner and began to weep.

"Sometimes I think I can still smell 'em now," he said. "No matter how much I drink, I can still smell 'em."

"He's crazy," Julia whispered.

"I think it's post-traumatic stress disorder," Isabel said. "I read an article about it. Any of us would have it if we had to look at what he saw."

The sheriff came back again, this time with a woman.

"Okay, Charlie," he said as he opened the padlock. "The missus is here to bring you home. Try to stay off the booze, will ya?"

Charlie's wife had a sad look in her eyes as she took him by the elbow and led him away.

"It was nice meetin' you young 'uns," Charlie said as he left. "You all stay out of trouble now."

The sheriff locked the cell door again and walked Charlie and his wife out of the jail.

"Maybe he'll let us go, too," Isabel said hopefully.

"Don't hold your breath," David told her. "He thinks we tried to shoot the president. He's not gonna just let us out of here."

A few minutes went by before the sheriff returned. He looked all flustered, like he had just seen a ghost.

"You got a visitor," he told the kids.

There was a boy standing behind the sheriff, and behind the boy stood a tall man in a stovepipe hat.

CHAPTER 20

THE DECISION

ON THE OTHER SIDE OF THE BARS, NOT MORE than three feet away, were President Abraham Lincoln and his son Tad. The Flashback Four stood there, eyes wide and mouths hanging open.

"That's them, Papa!" Tad told his father. "Those are the kids I was telling you about. They said they would give me a toy after your speech today. They *promised*."

"My good man," Lincoln said to the sheriff, "might I have a few moments in private with these young-sters?"

"Certainly, Mr. President," the sheriff replied, not quite sure if he should salute, bow, or do both. "Of course. Anything you want, sir."

The sheriff backed away, never taking his eyes off the president. Lincoln pulled a chair up next to the cell and sat down. Tad, who seemed restless, pointed his toy gun at the Flashback Four and pretended to fire it at each of them.

Close up, Abraham Lincoln looked older than his fifty-four years. His eyes were deep set, making them look darker. His face was furrowed, and his hair was graying at the temples. He had a melancholy look.

You've probably heard that the pressure of being the leader of the free world ages a president. Well, Lincoln had more pressure on him than *any* of them. The Civil War started just a month after he took office. It would end six days after his death. He had suffered much personal tragedy. Tad's older brother, Willie, had died the previous year, from typhoid fever. Another son, Eddie, had died as a toddler years earlier. It should come as no surprise that Abraham Lincoln's wife, Mary, suffered from mental problems. The president himself had variola, a mild form of smallpox.

And yet, behind the sadness, there was a kindness and gentleness in his face, too. The man had a subtle smile, like the *Mona Lisa*.

"So," he said, clearing his throat, "I have been informed that you youngsters are in a heap of trouble. Something about pointing a device of some sort in my direction. And my son here tells me you have been following us around. I figured I'd do a little investigation of my own. What have you got to say for yourselves?"

It was one thing to see the man speaking in front of a large crowd at the doorstep of the Wills house, or from the stage at the cemetery. But here he was— *Abraham Lincoln*—sitting a few feet away and staring into the faces of Luke, Isabel, Julia, and David. He was the most famous president of the United States, and arguably the most famous man in the *world*. It was intimidating. None of the kids knew what to say.

"Cat got your tongues?" Lincoln said. "Well, I've

always believed it's better to remain silent and be thought a fool than to speak out and remove all doubt."

"We . . . uh . . . well . . . ," Luke finally stammered, "it's hard to explain, sir."

"We come from the future," Julia blurted out.

"I beg your pardon?" asked the president.

"The thing is, we live in the twenty-first century," Julia told him. "We live in the future."

The rest of the Flashback Four rolled their eyes. There was no point in telling Julia to keep quiet.

"I know just one thing of the future," the president replied. "It comes only one day at a time."

"Well, here's what happened, Mr. President," Julia continued. "This billionaire lady named Chris Zandergoth built a smartboard—do you know what a smartboard is? It doesn't matter. Anyway, the smartboard can zap people to any place, any time. It's really cool. And Miss Z—we call her Miss Z—is obsessed with collecting photos of great moments in history, y'know? She wants to start a museum filled with them. And she's dying, so she's kind of in a hurry. She sent us back here with a digital camera to take a picture of you giving the Gettysburg Address. I swear, we would never shoot you. We would never shoot *anybody*."

From the moment Julia said "smartboard," Lincoln

had no idea what she was talking about.

"You spin quite a yarn, young lady," he told her, shaking his head. "That reminds *me* of a story."

"Not another story, Papa!" Tad said, groaning.

"Hush, Taddie," the president replied. "You see, what happened was that about five years back, I was ambling down the street in Springfield. Do you know Springfield? It's a town in Illinois. It doesn't matter. I was walking down the street when an odd-looking gentleman stopped me and pointed a revolver at my face. Well, I quickly realized that resistance would be unwise. Trying to remain calm, I asked the gentleman what was the problem."

The president had a gleam in his eye as he told the story.

"The odd-looking gentleman told me he'd sworn to himself that if he ever came across an uglier man than himself, he would shoot him on the spot," Lincoln continued. "So I told the man to go ahead and shoot me. Because if I was uglier than him, I wouldn't want to live."

Lincoln slapped his thigh and chuckled quietly. His face seemed happier now. It was like he used humor to mask his sadness.

"That's not funny, Papa," said Tad.

"Please believe us, Mr. President," Luke said. "We didn't come to shoot you. We came to shoot a *photograph* of you. It was just a misunderstanding."

Lincoln sat back in the chair and was quiet for a few seconds as he mulled over the situation.

"What do you reckon we should do with them, Taddie?" he asked his son.

David closed his eyes for a moment and said a silent prayer. He couldn't believe his fate was in the hands of Tad Lincoln, of all people. Luke, Isabel, and Julia were silently pleading with Tad with their eyes.

"I say we court-martial 'em, Papa," Tad said. "We should charge 'em with treason and sentence 'em to be shot at sunrise. Then we should bury 'em in the rose garden at the White House, like I did with my army doll, Jack."

Luke gulped.

"Hmm," said the president, stroking his beard. "That judgment deserves serious consideration, son. But I must say, it has been my experience that young 'uns who have no vices have very few virtues. In my boyhood days, I did many a foolish thing. I'm glad I was given a chance to redeem myself. Malice toward none, and charity for all. That's what I say. When this miserable war is concluded, should the Union emerge victorious, I will do the same for the Confederacy."

"Does this mean—" said Isabel.

"I am prepared to offer the four of you a full and binding presidential pardon," Lincoln said.

Whew! The Flashback Four breathed a collective sigh of relief.

"I will inform the sheriff of my decision on our way out," said Lincoln, "and then you will be free to go."

"Thank you! Thank you!" the kids said over and over again, just to make sure the president understood their gratitude.

"I do the very best I know how, the very best I can," Lincoln said as he got up and took Tad by the hand, "and I mean to keep on doing so until the end."

The sheriff came over to escort the president and his son from the jail. Just before he was out of earshot, Julia ran to the bars and shouted after him.

"Oh, Mr. President!" she yelled. "Don't go to Ford's Theatre!"

Lincoln just shook his head and walked away.

CHAPTER 21

THE SHOT

AFTER LINCOLN AND HIS SON LEFT, THE SHERIFF took his sweet time getting back to the cell where the kids were being held. He was on the street outside the jail, trying to make chitchat with the president.

"I wish he'd hurry up and get back here," Isabel said. "We need to be at the square by three o'clock. Anybody know what time it is?"

There was no way to check the time. There were no clocks on the wall, and no windows that would allow them to see the sun in the sky. But if Edward Everett had begun his speech at noon, and Lincoln had started his speech around two o'clock, it had to be getting close to three.

Finally, the sheriff returned. He took a set of keys off his belt.

"If I had my druthers, you bad eggs would rot here for a good long time," he said as he opened the padlock. "But by orders of the president of the United States himself, you are pardoned for your crimes. So I reckon you're free to go."

"Thanks!" David said as he pushed open the cell door. "Hey, can you tell us what time it is?"

"You mean *now*?" asked the sheriff.

David really wanted to reply, "Of *course* I mean now, you dope! What *other* time could I possibly mean?"

What David actually said was, "Yes, sir, *now*."

The kids watched impatiently as the sheriff reached into his pants pocket and pulled out a large round watch that was connected to a chain. He didn't own a regular watch. Nobody did. It would be five years until a Swiss watch maker would invent the modern wristwatch. If you don't believe me, look it up.

Slowly, the sheriff opened the metal cover of his pocket watch.

"Um, we're kind of in a hurry," Julia said, rolling her eyes.

"Hold your horses, missy," said the sheriff. "I'm sure that wherever it is you need to go can wait a few minutes. Now let me see here. The big hand is on the eleven and the little hand is on the—"

"It's five minutes to three!" Luke shouted, looking over the sheriff's shoulder.

"We only have five minutes!" yelled Isabel.

"Let's go!" shouted Luke.

They sprinted out of the jail, almost knocking down a little girl who was playing hopscotch on the sidewalk. It took a moment to get his bearings, but quickly Luke figured out which direction led back to Baltimore Street, and the square in the center of town.

The street was still crowded with people, but now most of them were walking *away* from the cemetery and toward the Gettysburg railroad station, which was a block north of the square. For many people, it would be a long ride home.

It was 2:57 when the Flashback Four got to Zerfing Alley, just a block from the square. It looked like they were going to make it with time leftover. That's when two boys ran in front of them, blocking their path.

"Oh no, not *them* again!" Julia said when she spotted the boys.

"Well, hello again, ladies!" the taller of the boys said. "I reckon we can't stop bumpin' into each other, can we? It must be fate."

"Perhaps you ladies would like to—"

"Can't talk!" Isabel shouted, shoving the boys aside. "Go boil your shirts!"

The Flashback Four ran up the street, leaving the boys staring at them, dumbfounded.

It was 2:59 when Luke, David, Isabel, and Julia arrived, breathlessly, at the square.

"Where are we supposed to go?" David asked.

"All Miss Z told us was to be in the middle of the square at three o'clock sharp," Luke replied.

In the middle of the square was a flagpole, with the American flag whipping in the breeze above. Without saying a word, the kids surrounded the pole, taking positions north, south, east, and west. Luke took Isabel's hand, Isabel took David's, David took Julia's, and Julia took Luke's.

Clang . . . clang . . . clang . . .

All the church bells in town began ringing to announce the new hour.

"This is it," Luke said, closing his eyes.

"She better come through," said David.

• • •

On the twenty-third floor of the John Hancock Tower in Boston, Miss Z and Mrs. Vader looked at the clock on the wall.

"It's three o'clock," Mrs. Vader said with a sigh.

"I guess it's time to reel them in," said Miss Z.

She was worried. She had wanted to "reel them in" a half hour earlier, when Isabel stopped responding to texts. She felt that something may have gone wrong. Maybe the kids were in trouble. But she wanted to give them every opportunity to complete their mission and get to the square by the prearranged time.

Miss Z typed a series of commands on her computer keyboard and hit the Enter key.

Bzzzzzzzzzzzzzz.

The screen on the Board lit up. Five bands of brilliant color appeared, separate at first and then coming together as one hot, white light.

"Here they come!" said Miss Z. "Right on schedule!"

The band of light jumped off the Board with a crackle as it stretched a few feet away from the surface. Then the humming sound kicked in. The floor was vibrating. It felt like the whole building was coming apart.

• • •

"It's happening!" said Julia, squinting and shielding her face. "We're going back!"

"I feel it!" David said. "I feel myself making the transformation!"

They were flickering on and off now. They didn't dare look at one another. They just held hands tightly for support.

In Boston, the Board was flashing like a strobe, illuminating bits and pieces of David, Luke, Isabel, and Julia. They were partly in the twenty-first century and partly in the nineteenth. The Board was struggling to fuse them into one.

On the square, a few people noticed that something unusual was going on around the flagpole. Some men came running over, but they were stopped in their tracks by the explosion of light and smoke that filled the air.

"What's happen—" was the last thing any of the Flashback Four said in 1863.

And then they vanished.

• • •

There was a burst of intense, white light in Miss Z's office. She and Mrs. Vader shielded their eyes. And then the light was gone.

The Flashback Four were back.

"We *made* it!" Luke shouted.

They hugged one another, crying tears of joy. David got down on his knees and kissed the floor.

"Welcome back!" said Mrs. Vader. "Are you kids okay?"

"I think so," Isabel said, speaking for the group.

"So what happened?" Miss Z asked. "I was getting worried about you. Why did you stop responding to my texts? Where's the TTT? Where's the camera? Did you get the shot? I'm anxious to see it!"

Luke, Julia, David, and Isabel looked at one another for a few seconds, each one waiting for somebody else to do the talking. Finally, Luke stepped forward.

"The shot . . . ," he said, trying to find the right words. "Yeah, funny thing about the shot. It's kind of a long story. . . ."

I know what you're thinking, reader. You're wondering what is going to happen next. Will Miss Z be furious with them? Will the kids be punished for returning without the camera or the TTT? Will she give them another chance? Will she fire them and hire a new Flashback Four? Or will she give up her dream to create a new museum of great moments in history?

As they say, time will tell. You'll just have to wait until the *next* adventure of the Flashback Four.

FACTS & FICTIONS

Everything in this book is true, except for the stuff I made up. It's only fair to tell you which is which.

First, the true stuff. The facts about Abraham Lincoln and the Gettysburg Address are true. I visited Gettysburg and also got a lot of information from excellent books such as *The Gettysburg Gospel* by Gabor Boritt, *Lincoln at Gettysburg* by Garry Wills, *Lincoln's Gettysburg Address* by Orton H. Carmichael, and *Gettysburg Remembers President Lincoln: Eyewitness Accounts of November 1863* by Linda Giberson Black.

It's also true that there are no existing images of Abraham Lincoln delivering the Gettysburg Address. But if you go to YouTube and search for "Gettysburg Address," you'll find many versions of other people reading the speech.

Now, the stuff I made up. Needless to say, Miss Z and the Flashback Four do not exist, and neither does the Board. Too bad, huh?

Abraham Lincoln's son Tad was ten years old in 1863, but he was *not* at Gettysburg. In fact, he was sick at home in Washington, and the president almost didn't make the trip himself because of Tad's illness. Two of Tad's brothers had already died, and Mrs. Lincoln begged the president to stay home. But he was determined to give the speech, and thankfully, he did.

Tad might very well have been in Gettysburg if he hadn't taken sick. He would frequently accompany his father to inspect the troops or go on trips. The two went to Richmond, Virginia, together and toured the Confederate capital just a few days after the Union army took over the city.

Tad was a fascinating boy. He didn't read or write and did not attend school until after his father died. Today, he would almost certainly be diagnosed with one learning disability or another. He was known for being impulsive and unrestrained, but also cheerful and mischievous. Tad would hold yard sales on the White House lawn, where he would sell his father's suits and his mother's dresses. He also made money for himself by charging visitors a nickel to meet the president. He loved all things military. One time he constructed a fort on the White House roof. On another occasion, he opened fire on the president's cabinet with a toy cannon. I just *had* to put him in the story.

Ten days after Tad turned twelve, his father was assassinated. Tad himself died just six years later, probably from tuberculosis.

John Wilkes Booth was also not at Gettysburg. I just couldn't resist sticking him in there for the sake of the story.

DON'T MISS THE NEXT ADVENTURE!

Turn the page for a sneak peek at the Flashback Four's most dangerous mission yet—a journey to the deck of the doomed *Titanic* for a shot of the sinking ship.

INTRODUCTION

IT WAS TWENTY MINUTES BEFORE MIDNIGHT when steel touched ice.

The date: April 14, 1912.

The place: the north Atlantic Ocean, about 370 miles southeast of Newfoundland.

It was cold outside. So cold. As cold as ice.

The ocean was flat and calm that night, almost like a sheet of glass. The largest ship in the world at the time—the *Titanic*—had nearly completed its maiden voyage. It sliced through the water at top speed, close to twenty-four miles per hour.

The sky was clear, cloudless, and almost moonless,

except for a tiny sliver. But the stars were bright and sometimes shooting. So peaceful. It must have been tempting to take one's eye off the distant horizon and gaze up at the star show above.

Maybe that's what happened. Maybe the lookout glanced up and saw a shooting star. He couldn't take his eyes off it. And then, when he returned his gaze to the horizon moments later, he saw it directly in front of him—an enormous mountain of ice.

In Greek mythology, the Titans were a race of giant gods with incredible strength who ruled the Golden Age. That's how the *Titanic* got its name.

It would seem like no contest—frozen water versus hard steel. But it was the steel that broke, not the ice.

The iceberg towered sixty feet high, and that was just the part of it that was above the waterline. It was eight times larger *below* the surface, and four times the size of the *Titanic* steaming directly toward it—a *million* tons of ice.

Everything happened so fast after that. The lookout turned around and frantically rang the emergency bell three times.

"Hard starboard!" somebody on the bridge shouted almost immediately.

But it was far too late. It's not easy to turn around

a vessel that's nine hundred feet long and weighs over forty-six *thousand* tons. It takes time, and that was one thing in short supply. *Titanic* was only a quarter mile away from the iceberg and closing fast.

It's easy to say now, but it probably would have been better if the *Titanic* hadn't turned at all. It should have just rammed the iceberg head-on. The front of the ship was designed to take a hit. It might have survived the damage. The sides of the ship were much more fragile.

Just thirty-seven seconds after the emergency bell rang, steel touched ice on the front right side of *Titanic*—the starboard side. The impact was ten feet above the keel, but well below the waterline.

There was no crash. No jolt. It appeared to be a glancing blow. A little bump. Harmless. *Titanic* didn't even stop moving forward. The iceberg didn't break apart. It was like . . . two ships passing in the night.

But the hull of the *Titanic*—like any large ship—was made of hundreds of overlapping steel plates, each of them just an inch and a half thick. These plates were held in place by iron rivets. The rivets were small, just an inch thick and three inches long. When ice touched steel, something had to give.

It was the rivets. Iron isn't as strong as steel. One at

a time the rivets popped off. *Pop. Pop. Pop.* The heads of the rivets had been sliced off, like mushrooms.

The hull didn't open up like a zipper or a can opener, the way it has sometimes been described. Without rivets to hold them in place, the steel plates that lined the ship were roughly shoved aside, like a toddler ripping the wrapping paper off a birthday present.

Water gushed in the gash, four hundred tons of it a minute. The sixteen "watertight" compartments that lined the hull began to fill.

Only some of the passengers on board heard the rumbling, grinding noise below deck. Most of them were asleep and didn't notice a thing.

And then, just like that, it was over. The iceberg floated on by as if nothing unusual had happened. It was chipped in a few places but none the worse for wear.

In less than ten seconds, the damage had been done to *Titanic*. That's all it took. The "unsinkable" ship was fatally injured. And the unthinkable was about to happen.

CHAPTER 1

THE FLASHBACK FOUR

TO TELL THIS STORY THE WAY IT SHOULD BE TOLD, we need to go back, or, I should say, *forward* in time.

The story begins in the present day, in the left field bleachers at Fenway Park in Boston, Massachusetts. The Red Sox are playing the Yankees, but the ball game is secondary to what's going on in the stands.

Sitting in the front row above Fenway's famous Green Monster are four sixth-grade students. You already met them if you read a book called *Flashback Four: The Lincoln Project.* If you haven't read it, you really should. If you *have* read it, all the better.

It's impossible and really unfair, of course, to sum up a human being in just a few sentences. But at the same time, you don't want to sit through page after page of character description. You'll get to know these young people better as the story goes on. But for now we're all busy, so here goes . . .

Luke: A big white kid from the streets of Dorchester. He's got a touch of ADD and a heart of gold.
Julia: A prep school blonde who likes money, clothes, and taking risks, maybe a little too much.
David: A tall, thin African American kid who likes to laugh but knows when to get serious.
Isabel: A studious kid originally from the Dominican Republic who plays by the rules, and expects to be rewarded for it.

Two boys. Two girls. They call themselves the Flashback Four. They didn't know each other until quite recently. They go to separate schools. But they bonded, as often happens when people are thrown into a life-or-death situation together. In surviving the Lincoln Project they became friends, and they'd decided to get together to talk about their future . . . and the past.

Luke and David are serious Red Sox fans, but that's not how the Flashback Four found themselves in

Fenway Park that day. They got the tickets from Julia's father, a wealthy Boston hedge fund manager.

I know what you're thinking. There can't be a lot of money in managing hedges. But Julia's dad did quite well for himself and had season tickets. Taking his wealthy clients to Fenway was good for business. He had four tickets he wasn't using on this particular day and offered them to Julia.

This is a girl who doesn't know the difference between a foul ball and a grand slam. But she knew the boys would appreciate it, and she thought it would be a nice way to get the group together after they got back from their first adventure.

"Free tickets to see the Sox play the Yankees," Luke said, high-fiving David as they found their seats. "It doesn't get much better than this."

"Baseball is such a *bore*." Julia yawned. "What do they have to eat around here?"

Neither team scored in the first inning, but the Flashback Four weren't paying much attention to the game anyway. They were still recovering from what had happened at Gettysburg.

To put it simply, they had been recruited by a billionaire—Miss Chris Zandergoth—who had earned her fortune developing an online dating site called

Findamate. She spent a big chunk of that fortune creating an interactive smartboard that could function as a time-traveling device.

It was simply called the Board. If you think the smartboard in *your* school is high-tech, you ain't seen nothin'. This was a smarter board. Don't even try to understand the technology. It's for super techies.

Anyway, Miss Zandergoth sent the Flashback Four to 1863 with a mission—to take a photograph of Abraham Lincoln delivering the Gettysburg Address. Miss Z, as she is called, has an obsession with photos of historical events, and especially historical events that have never been photographed before. There is no existing photo of Lincoln giving that speech. Go ahead, look it up. Or just take my word for it.

Luke, Julia, Isabel, and David *were* able to witness the Gettysburg Address in person, but unfortunately they were *not* able to bring back a photo of Lincoln delivering it. In fact, they were attacked and jailed, and poor Julia even had the misfortune to step in a pile of 1863 dog poop. To tell you the truth, the Flashback Four were lucky to get back to the present day with their lives. If you want the full story, again, read the book.

The Red Sox took the field to start the second inning. Luke had just come back to the seats with hot dogs for everybody.

"Y'know," Isabel said as she took a bite, "with the Board, we could travel to *any* moment in time and take a picture of it."

"Obviously," David said.

"Where do you think Miss Z will send us next?" Luke asked.

The possibilities were endless. Photography was perfected in 1839. So no photos exist of *anything* that happened before that year. They could go back to Christmas night of 1776 and photograph George Washington with his troops, crossing the Delaware to launch a surprise attack on the British army at Trenton. Or they could go back to 1510 and photograph Michelangelo as he painted his masterpiece on the ceiling of the Sistine Chapel. Or they could go back to prehistoric times and snap a photo of a dinosaur.

"You know what would be cool?" Isabel said. "We could take a picture of the Wright Brothers flying the first airplane at Kitty Hawk, North Carolina."

"I'm pretty sure there's already a picture of that," Luke said. "I think I saw it in a book once."

Luke was right. Orville and Wilbur Wright very carefully documented their experiments with flying machines, and they had a member of the Kill Devil Hills Lifesaving Station snap a photo just as Orville lifted off the ground for the first time on December 17, 1903. The flight lasted all of twelve seconds. It was one of the most famous photographs of the twentieth century. So there was no point in trying to take *that* picture.

It only took a few seconds for Julia to find it on her smartphone. . . .

The first batter for the Yankees grounded out, and the second one singled up the middle.

The Flashback Four discussed a few other possibilities for photos. Amazingly, nobody had thought to take a photograph of generals Ulysses S. Grant and Robert E. Lee signing the agreement to end the Civil War. There was no photograph of Amelia Earhart crash-landing her plane on a remote island in the Pacific Ocean, of course. A photo of the Founding Fathers signing the Declaration of Independence would be amazing. Many famous events in history can only be imagined from paintings that were made of them.

As the next Yankee stepped up to the plate, a message flashed on the scoreboard. None of the Flashback Four noticed it at first. . . .

DID YOU KNOW . . .

the message read,

FENWAY PARK IS THE OLDEST MAJOR LEAGUE BALLPARK IN AMERICA?

"Who cares?" muttered Julia, glancing up at the scoreboard as she took a bite of her hot dog.

IT OPENED ON APRIL 20, 1912.

"Big deal," muttered Julia.

HERE ARE A FEW OTHER FAMOUS EVENTS THAT HAPPENED IN 1912....

- **January: The Republic of China was established**
- **February: Arizona became the 48th state**
- **March: The Dixie Cup was invented**
- **April: The *Titanic* sank in the Atlantic Ocean**

The word *Titanic* caught Isabel's eye as she glanced up at the scoreboard. The story of the *Titanic* was one of those things that just about everybody knew, even though it happened so long ago and it isn't taught in schools. It was one of the most famous events of the twentieth century. Isabel had seen the 1997 movie *Titanic* during a sleepover at a friend's house. She nudged Julia, who Googled the word *Titanic* on her smartphone.

"It says here that the *Titanic* sank on April 15, 1912," she said. "That was just five days before this ballpark opened."

Nobody said anything for a minute or two. The Yankee batter took a couple pitches out of the strike zone, and then grounded into a double play, throwing the Red Sox fans into a frenzy. David turned to Luke.

"Are you thinking what I'm thinking?" he asked.

"I think I'm thinking *exactly* what you're thinking," Luke replied. "Is there a photo of the *Titanic* sinking?"

Isabel looked it up on her phone.

"No," she reported. "It says here that there are plenty of pictures of the *Titanic* before it set sail, but no photos of it actually sinking."

"Why not?" asked Julia. "They had cameras in 1912."

"All the cameras that were on board probably went down with the ship," David guessed, "and the people in the lifeboats couldn't bring anything with them. They were just trying to stay alive."

"It was women and children first," Isabel noted. "Maybe in those days, women weren't allowed to *use* cameras. We couldn't even vote until 1920."

The Yankee batter struck out to end the inning, causing the crowd to erupt in cheers, but none of the Flashback Four were paying attention to the game anymore.

"Can you imagine how cool it would be to sail on the *Titanic*?" asked Luke.

"I would do it," Julia said. "We would get to hobnob with all those rich society people."

"Count me out, guys," Isabel announced. "Too dangerous for me."

She had pulled out her own phone and was scrolling through various websites about the *Titanic*. She learned that the ship was going too fast that night. That the captain ignored multiple warnings about icebergs in the area. The rivets holding the ship together should have been made of steel instead of iron. There weren't enough lifeboats for all the passengers. The lookout didn't even have binoculars, because they were locked in a locker and nobody had the key! So many things had gone wrong, and fifteen hundred people had died.

"What, do you want to spend your whole life staring at a cell phone?" David told her. "Come on. We could do this. YOLO. You only live once."

"And you only *die* once!" Isabel replied. "Are you crazy? It would be a suicide mission! Most of the people on the *Titanic died*, you know. We almost got killed just going to Gettysburg. Do you think we're going to survive on a ship that's going to sink?"

"Yeah, we'll survive," Luke said calmly. "Because we have something none of those *Titanic* passengers had."

"What?" asked Isabel.

"The Board," Luke said, looking at her. "As soon